"Mommy, look there's a dog! A real dog!"

"That's Cleopatra, but we call her Cleo," Johnny said. "Come on, Kenny. She's been lonely and needs a friend."

Rachel sensed he wasn't just talking about the dog. That he had figured out more about her from their initial meeting than she'd intended to reveal.

No…that wasn't possible.

"Cleo was a stray I found on the side of the road," he said. "She'd been abandoned and abused. She needs someone to love her."

Tears burned Rachel's throat. He sounded so sincere.

And somehow he'd picked up on the fact that her son needed stability. Peace. Normalcy.

She let him guide her toward the dining hall. They would stay, she decided.

But at the first sign of trouble, that her ex had followed them, they'd hit the road and never look back.

RITA HERRON

CERTIFIED COWBOY

TORONTO NEW YORK LONDON
AMSTERDAM PARIS SYDNEY HAMBURG
STOCKHOLM ATHENS TOKYO MILAN MADRID
PRAGUE WARSAW BUDAPEST AUCKLAND

To a great friend and writer,
Delores Fossen—thanks for talking up the cowboys!

Recycling programs
for this product may
not exist in your area.

ISBN-13: 978-0-373-74644-6

CERTIFIED COWBOY

Copyright © 2012 by Rita B. Herron

ABOUT THE AUTHOR

Award-winning author Rita Herron wrote her first book when she was twelve, but didn't think real people grew up to be writers. Now she writes so she doesn't have to get a *real* job. A former kindergarten teacher and workshop leader, she traded her storytelling to kids for romance, and now she writes romantic comedies and romantic suspense. She lives in Georgia with her own romance hero and three kids. She loves to hear from readers, so please write her at P.O. Box 921225, Norcross, GA 30092-1225, or visit her website at www.ritaherron.com.

Books by Rita Herron

CAST OF CHARACTERS

Johnny Long—This sexy rodeo star turned rancher has problems of his own. But when danger strikes, he wants to protect a single mom and her son. Only she has secrets in her eyes, and Johnny must protect his heart.

Rachel Presley—She's running for her life. Will her ex-husband catch her in the end?

Kenny Presley—The little boy craves a home and a family. Will he find it at the Bucking Bronc Lodge?

Rex Presley—How far will he go to get his wife back? And when he does, will he kill her as he vowed?

Rich Copeland—The rich rancher who owns the spread next to the Bucking Bronc Lodge is adamantly against housing troubled kids next door. Would he sabotage the ranch and endanger lives to make the ranch fail?

Ricardo Mendez—The orphaned teenager is out to cause trouble. Could he be making problems at the ranch?

Frank Dunham—An ex-con who's working at the ranch and a friend of Carter Flagstone's, a man who had a vendetta against Johnny and his friend Brandon. Would Carter pay Frank to cause trouble as a way of getting revenge?

Dewey Burgess—He attacked Rachel in the barn. Did he have his own agenda, or is he working for Rachel's ex?

Chapter One

Rachel Presley was suffocating.

"I told you I'd never let you go."

Her ex-husband's sinister voice made her body convulse with fear. Rex had found her.

Again.

"No," she whispered in a raw voice. "Please..." She tried to pry his hands from around her neck, but his grip tightened, and his fingernails dug into her throat, closing off her windpipe.

She jerked awake, trembling. Her hands felt clammy, her throat raw, her stomach heaving.

It couldn't be real. She was dreaming again. Having another one of the terrifying nightmares that had dogged her since she'd left Rex.

But a wet tongue trailed a path down the side of her face. A very real wet tongue. "I'd forgotten how beautiful you look when you're sleeping, Rach."

Nausea flooded her. How had he found her this

time? She'd covered her bases, changed her name again, hadn't left a paper trail behind...

But the acrid scent of sweat and whiskey breath told her that she hadn't been smart enough.

Rex's heavy weight pressed her into the mattress, and stirred her panic to a frenzy.

"Just tell me you're sorry and come back to me, Rachel." Another swipe of his tongue and he ground his crotch into hers. "You want me," he murmured into her hair. "I can feel it."

"No," she whispered. But her efforts to escape were cut off as his hands tightened around her throat.

"Yes, you do. Say it." He kneed her legs apart with his and rubbed the rough stubble of his jaw against her face. He'd always thought it was funny to hear the rasp of his whiskers scraping her delicate jaw. And he'd taken pride in the whisker burns he left behind. He liked to mark her, brand her like a piece of cattle, so any man who looked her way recognized that she belonged to him.

"Our son needs me, too," Rex murmured. "And I intend to be there for him. To teach him how to be a man."

Over her dead body.

Ever since she'd left Rex, she'd been prepared for him to find her. Attack her. Beat her up. Try to kill her.

He had once before.

That was the reason she'd run. And bought a .38.

"After we make love, you can whip us up a batch of pancakes," Rex said. "Kenny will be happy to see me, won't he, Rach?"

The thought of Rex touching, *fathering* her precious son sent rage through her, and she summoned every ounce of strength she possessed. Kenny would never be subjected to Rex's violent mood swings.

But Rex had gained weight and he was even heavier than she remembered. She had to use her wits to gain advantage long enough to retrieve her gun.

"Rex, please…you're choking me." She lifted her hips slightly as if she was warming to his touch, and in the moonlight streaking the room she saw a slow lecherous smile spread across his face. Rex was such a narcissistic man that he still believed she'd fall for his charms.

"That's it, baby. Show me you still love me." His hands slid down her throat to her breasts, then he shifted slightly, ready to shuck his jeans.

Taking advantage of the moment to strike, she raised her knee and slammed it into his groin, then shoved him backward with all her might. Rex bellowed in pain and shock, and she reached sideways below the mattress and grabbed her gun.

He lunged at her, but she flicked off the safety and pointed the barrel at his chest.

"Move and I'll shoot."

Shock made his eyes bulge. "You wouldn't, Rachel. You're too soft."

"You changed that," she said sharply. Keeping the gun trained on him, she slowly pushed herself up on the bed and slid off the side. He started to move toward her, but she shook her head and cocked the trigger, then yanked open the drawer to her nightstand and removed a pair of handcuffs she'd bought at a pawn store.

"One inch," she said. "And you're dead."

His jaw hardened to steel and he froze, but the menacing look in his eyes grew fierce and deadly.

"You wouldn't shoot the father of your son," he said, although his voice had a tremor to it this time.

Good, let him know what it felt like to be afraid.

"Now sit down in that desk chair," she said between clenched teeth.

His eyes narrowed, but he gave a cocky shrug as if he thought it was a game. Then she pressed the gun to his temple and tossed the handcuffs into his lap. "Handcuff yourself to the chair. Now."

He shot blades of steel from his eyes and cursed violently, but did as she said.

"You're going to regret this," he growled.

"The only thing I regret is marrying you." Still keeping the gun aimed at him, she tugged on her jacket, grabbed her purse, then ran to get Kenny, tucking the .38 in her handbag so he wouldn't see it. He was asleep in his bed and looked so innocent and cozy snuggled with his blanket and stuffed puppy that she hated to disturb him.

But they had to go.

He stirred as she lifted him in her arms. "Mommy?" He blinked and glanced around his room, confused.

"It's okay, sweetie. We're taking a little trip. Go back to sleep."

She wrapped him in the blanket, tucked his stuffed animal under his arm, then ran toward the den. The chair clanged against the floor in the bedroom, then Rex's grating voice shattered the air.

"I'll kill you when I find you, Rachel. You'll never get away from me. Never!"

Rachel's throat clogged with fear, but she forged ahead and ran out the door. A breeze kicked up, stirring leaves and dust around her as she settled Kenny in the backseat and buckled him in. Just as she climbed in the driver's side and shut the door, Rex ran onto the front porch, dragging the chair behind him. His arms were still chained to the wood, and he was cursing and raging like a bull tied in a pen.

Grateful she'd kept a suitcase for her and Kenny packed in the trunk, she cranked the engine and stepped on the gas. Then she gunned the engine and ripped down the dirt road, praying she could outrun him this time.

If he caught her again, there was no doubt in her mind that he'd kill her.

JOHNNY LONG HAD TO MAKE one more attempt to help his old friend Carter Flagstone clear his name.

He just hoped to hell Carter didn't refuse to see him as he had the last time he'd tried to visit the jail.

The sprawling ranch faded in his vision as he headed toward the state prison, and his thoughts turned back to the meeting with Brody Bloodworth, the founder of the Bucking Bronc Lodge. The ranch was designed to give troubled boys a second chance through working with animals, ranch hands and cowboys, and reminded him of how he, Carter and Brandon Woodstock had all grown up.

He admired Brody and his plans and appreciated the fact he'd given his sister, Kim, a job, yet Johnny had sworn never to put himself in the limelight again. And spearheading the rodeo Brody wanted to raise money for the summer camps would do exactly that. Worse, using his name could backfire in all their faces.

Still, the idea of a rodeo for a bunch of needy,

troubled kids, kids like he had once been, sent an adrenaline rush through him that he hadn't felt in a long time. If it hadn't been for the rodeo, he might never have pulled himself out of the gutter. But fame and fortune came at a price.

And the events of that last year, the way the media had turned on him, had almost destroyed him. Still, as a kid, channeling his anger and energy into penning, roping cows and riding had saved his life.

That and his friendship with Brandon and Carter. They had been like the Three Musketeers, growing up.

All from poor, dysfunctional homes. All rough-housing boys who liked to ride and cause trouble and skirt with the law. All had sorry daddies who'd beaten them. Mothers who'd done just as much damage by walking away, finding home in a bottle or just plain ignoring the abuse.

So they'd found each other, had watched each other's backs for years, even taken beatings for one another.

Until five years ago when everything had gone wrong.

When Carter had been arrested, he and Brandon had taken a good hard look at their own lives and decided it was time to grow up. Sure, they'd had bad childhoods. Lived in hellholes. Never had a family who gave a damn.

But they'd made a pact to show the world they weren't the white-trash losers the rich rancher kids had dubbed them.

Yet Carter had still wound up in jail. Not that Johnny believed he was guilty of the murder he'd been locked up for. Well, maybe he'd had a few doubts, but he really didn't think Carter was a cold-blooded killer....

Only, Carter had refused to talk and had begged him and Brandon to give him an alibi. A phony alibi.

If he wasn't guilty, why had he asked him and Brandon to lie?

Their refusal to commit perjury, circumstantial evidence, incompetent lawyers and a lowlife judge who might have been paid off had cost his friend his freedom.

Even worse, Carter claimed he and Brandon were getting revenge for his short fling with Johnny's sister, Kim. Brandon had dated Kim first, much to Johnny's consternation, then he'd broken her heart, which had caused tension between him and Brandon. On the rebound, she'd fallen into Carter's arms, which had ended badly for everyone, causing a rift between Brandon and Carter.

But Kim had suffered, as well, and Johnny had had to work to contain his own bitterness. His sister had been off-limits and both his friends had crossed the line.

But that wasn't the reason he hadn't lied for Carter.

Still, Carter had refused his visits and letters over the years.

Didn't Carter know that it hurt them to see him locked up? That they wanted justice, too?

He had to give it one more try.

But he fought a sense of guilt as he parked his pickup in front of the prison and reread the news article about Carter's father's death. How was Carter handling the news?

Ten minutes later, he'd made it through security, his nerves spiking as memories of being arrested needled him. He'd come so close to being locked in jail himself that he still half expected one of the rangers to snap a pair of handcuffs on him and throw him in a cell.

His stomach churned as he slid into the vinyl seat in the visiting area. It seemed like hours, but finally the metal door screeched open, and Carter shuffled through the door in handcuffs, his face pale and bruised, his lip busted, fresh scars on his arms. His eyes looked dull, his jaw set firm as he dropped into the seat on the other side of the Plexiglas. For a moment, Johnny didn't think he was going to look at him, then Carter leveled a sharp stare at him that felt like a knife piercing his gut.

"What do you want now?" Carter ground out.

Johnny swallowed and tried to control his anger. If Carter had just talked to him and told him the truth years ago, maybe they could have helped him.

Instead of rehashing that, though, he gestured to the news article. "I'm sorry about your old man."

Fresh pain and fury flickered across Carter's face, then he released a sarcastic laugh. "You know I didn't give a damn about that mean old cuss."

With good reason. The bastard had put plenty of bruises and scars on Carter. "He's still your old man."

"He was a drunk who hated my guts." Carter gripped his hands together and leaned closer to the microphone. "But he had a nice piece of ranch land, once." Carter's eyes narrowed suspiciously. "Is that why you're here? The rich and famous Johnny Long planning to buy up my old man's spread to add to his empire."

Johnny ground his teeth. "No, Carter. I came as a friend."

"I don't have any friends," Carter snapped. "I lost them years ago."

"That's not fair, Carter."

"What's not fair is that I've been stuck in this pit watching my daddy's spread go down the toilet while you and Brandon built your fortunes."

Johnny understood his need to vent, but he was still Carter's friend whether Carter liked it or not. "Is the property going into foreclosure?"

The chair clanked as Carter stood. "So you *are* here to see about buying it?"

"No," Johnny said quickly. "But I do have money, Carter, and if you need me to do something to keep the property from going into foreclosure, I will."

"I don't want your charity."

"Then what about a loan? We can come up with some kind of payback plan for when you're released—"

"For when I'm released?" Carter hissed. "Don't you get it, Johnny? I'm never getting out." Carter's voice was cold, but Johnny detected fear underlying it.

"There's parole," Johnny argued.

A look of defeat settled in Carter's eyes. "Even if I did make parole, I've got nothing. No way to keep the land. And no one in Texas is going to hire a convicted murderer."

Johnny started to say that he would, but before he could voice the thought, Carter shook his head in warning.

"Don't you dare," Carter snarled. "I don't want your pity. And I would never work for you." He turned and strode toward the door, the chains around his ankles rattling.

"I'll hire another attorney," Johnny said. "I'll find the best, Carter—"

Carter slowly turned around, his expression bitter. "Go to hell, Johnny."

Johnny silently cursed as the metal doors banged shut behind Carter. Damn. What good was having money if he couldn't use it to help his friend?

Johnny stood, frustrated, his stomach tied in knots. Maybe he couldn't do anything for Carter now, but there were kids at the Bucking Bronc Lodge who deserved his help. To hell with worrying about the press putting a negative slant on him.

Brody and the ranch needed him. He was going to start organizing that rodeo as soon as he got back.

"WHERE'RE WE GOING, Mommy?" Kenny clutched his stuffed puppy to him, his voice edged with worry. He'd obviously sensed her distress when he'd woken up in yet another strange motel and realized they were on the run again.

"To a big ranch, bud." Rachel tried to inject enthusiasm into her voice. "I think you're going to like it there."

And she would like the solitude, the distance

from the city, and the miles between her and Rex. Provided he hadn't already sniffed out their trail.

Kenny craned his neck to see out the window of the Jeep she'd traded her sedan for. "Are we there?"

"Almost." They'd passed San Antonio an hour earlier, and he'd been asking the same question since. Relief swept over her as she turned down a long, winding road, then spotted the welcome sign. "Look, it says BBL—the Bucking Bronc Lodge."

"They really got horses and I can ride one?" Kenny asked.

"Yes, they do. And there'll be lots of space to play outdoors."

"Maybe we can get a puppy here!" He hugged his stuffed toy. "A *real* one!"

Rachel shrugged. "Maybe." Although, having a pet made it harder to travel or pick up and move again if they had to. And she had no doubt they would at some time.

As they drove down the mile-long drive to the main house and headquarters of the operation, she admired the lush pastures, the stables and riding pens, the cattle grazing lazily around the pond, the horses galloping across the land, and her nerves settled somewhat. If anyone needed another chance, she and Kenny did.

This place was just isolated enough to provide a reprieve…

She only hoped they still had some positions open.

"Look, there's horses!" Kenny brightened, making guilt nag at Rachel. She wanted a home for Kenny so badly she could cry. But he hadn't had a place to call home in two years. And he barely remembered the house she'd shared with Rex.

Thank God. Hopefully that meant he'd forgotten the screaming and brutal fights.

A large two-story rustic log cabin with skylights to let in light, farmhouse decor, a metal bull outside on the lawn and fence posts designated for tying horses in front of the house appeared in her view, and her heart stuttered. A huge porch complete with rocking chairs and colorful flowers flanking the front made it feel homey and inviting. Then she spotted other log cabins strewn across the land, and realized the lodge was central to the operation but they also offered individual cabins, probably for guests or employees. From what she'd read, there were acres and acres of riding trails, ponds and camping sites for the campers.

This house, the sprawling ranch, the stables and rolling land, was the kind of place dreams were made on.

Only, she'd stopped dreaming a long time ago.

Still, she parked and grabbed her purse. Before she could go around to open the back door for Kenny, he'd unfastened his seat belt and jumped out. "Can I ride now?"

Rachel climbed from the vehicle. "No, not yet." Rachel led him up the stone pathway to the front porch. "Now remember, Mommy has to get a job here so we can stay. So be a good boy for me, okay? And remember our game. Right now our last name is Simmons. Rachel and Kenny Simmons."

He bobbed his head up and down. She knew the name change was confusing, but it was necessary, so she squeezed his hand, then knocked on the door.

A second later, the door opened, and Rachel could only gawk. A big rugged cowboy wearing a black Stetson with silver trim, chambray shirt, jeans, a belt buckle engraved with a bucking bull and black boots with rhinestone studs stared down at her. He was at least six-three, had shoulders so wide that he filled half the doorway, and crystal blue eyes that sparkled with a hint of the devil inside. Lady-killer eyes.

Eyes she recognized from magazine articles, newspaper stories and TV.

Johnny Long. Famous rodeo star. Bronco rider.

Barrel racer. Champion bull rider. You name it, Johnny Long had done and had won it.

He was also a notorious playboy. A man who wrecked women's hearts.

Suddenly her voice wouldn't work.

"Howdy," he said in a lazy Texas drawl. "Did you come to register your little boy for camp?"

Kenny pulled at her hand. "Mommy, can I do camp?"

Rachel struggled to pull herself together. "Actually, I...came to apply for a job."

"All right." His eyes cut over her, then he seemed to zero in on her neck, and the friendly gleam in his eyes died.

Rachel automatically adjusted the scarf she'd tied around her throat to hide the bruises Rex had left.

But it was too late. He had seen them.

Her heart hammered. If he thought she was in trouble, he probably wouldn't hire her.

Then where would she and Kenny go?

REX CURSED AS HE TORE through the small house where his wife had lived. It had taken him half an hour to cut the damn handcuffs apart with bolt cutters, then another ten to pick the stupid lock.

He rubbed at the angry red marks on his wrists. The damn bitch would be sorry for what she'd done.

He stormed through the bedroom, ripping apart

the bedding with his knife, then he slashed the mattress covering and pillows, shredding the insides just to purge his fury.

But his blood was still boiling.

Determined that she wouldn't escape him, he raked through the small desk in the corner, searching for any clue as to where she might take his son next. He'd been chasing her for months from one small Podunk town to another, from divey hotels to rental houses to cabins not fit for a dog to live in, much less his kid.

She was turning Kenny against him. His own son looked at him as if he was a monster just because of the filthy lies that came from that woman's mouth.

How could she do this to him?

She'd vowed to love him, to honor him and cherish him, but she'd turned on him. She'd told filthy lies about him. Used his son to bargain her way into earning sympathy from that snotty lawyer lady.

Hell, she'd probably spread her legs and slept with the bastard judge to get him to sign those damn divorce papers.

Both of them would pay for that.

Blind rage ate at him, and he jerked open the dresser drawers, yanking out the contents. Satin panties, bras, tank tops—he ripped them all to shreds and dropped the remnants on the tattered carpet. Again, he searched for a notepad, address book, brochure, anything that might tell him where she was running to this time, but found nothing except receipts for the cabin, which she'd paid for in cash.

She was learning not to leave a paper trail.

She'd pay for that, too.

Balling his hand into a fist, he raced to the kitchen and searched the drawers. No address or notes there, either.

But he found a hammer in a kitchen drawer and he slammed it against the counter, cracking the cheap surface, then used it to obliterate the glass-front china cabinet, breaking the door and smashing the dishes inside.

Then he went back to the bedroom and smashed the mirror above the dresser, then the bathroom mirror, watching as glass shattered and sprayed the floor.

His blood pounded through his veins as he headed back to his car. Heaving with unspent anger, he stepped outside in the night air. A smile curved his mouth as he removed the wedding ring she'd thrown back at him from his pocket and rubbed it between his fingers. The gold band was simple, but it was an unbroken circle, which symbolized how their lives were supposed to be entwined.

An image of Rachel wearing that white wedding dress the day they'd married at that little country chapel flashed in his mind, and he squeezed the ring so hard that his knuckles turned white.

He had put that ring on her finger and made her his wife. And she had agreed to love him until death parted them.

To hell with the judge.

Divorce papers couldn't separate them.

Only death would.

Chapter Two

Johnny gritted his teeth at the sight of the bruises on the woman's throat. Her long, curly black hair, which looked dyed, swirled around her neck, and she'd tied a scarf around it to hide the worst, but the purple-and-black marks were still visible and looked stark against her pale skin.

Someone had hurt her, bad.

Her husband? Boyfriend? Lover? Or a stranger?

His temper rose, his protective instincts kicking in. Having a younger sister had done that to him. Taught him to respect women, not to use his physical power to get what he wanted.

No matter what the press might have said.

He opened his mouth to ask her who had tried to choke her, but the wary look in her eyes and the way she quickly tried to cover up the bruises made him pause.

"My name is Rachel Simmons, and this is my son Kenny. I saw the ad in the paper," she said, straightening her spine.

He sensed she wanted to look tough, but he towered over her, and soaking wet, she probably didn't weigh a hundred and ten pounds.

"Right, a job," Johnny said, collecting himself. He glanced down at the little boy and immediately checked for bruises but didn't see any, so he breathed a sigh of relief. Still, the kid looked scared and kept his head bowed.

"Come on in."

Rachel nodded, and she and her little boy followed him through the entryway into one of the offices adjoining Brody's. Because all of the contributors had their own ranches to run and needed to keep in touch while they volunteered at the BBL, he'd designated several smaller offices for them to use, complete with state-of-the-art computer systems, faxes and phones.

Rachel looked surprised at the office furnishings. "Wow, I thought this was going to be a working ranch."

"It is," Johnny said. "Don't let this setup fool you. Outdoors, it's all ranching. But running an operation like the BBL requires organization, funding, volunteers, employees."

"Of course it does," she said. "It's a wonderful idea. The concept of helping kids in need through hard work and counseling, of giving them role models, is very admirable."

Finally, the little boy looked up at him, his

curiosity overcoming his fear. But his voice sounded timid. "Are you a real cowboy?"

Johnny smiled at the kid and nodded. "Yeah, I've been riding since I was born."

"You own all these horses here?" Kenny asked.

Johnny shook his head. "No, they belong to the Bucking Bronc. But I have horses and cattle on my ranch at home." He almost spouted off the impressive number of cattle he owned and the champion horse breeding he was so proud of, but decided now was not the time to brag.

Kenny's eyes widened. "I seen you before. You was on TV." He moved closer, tipping his head back and looking up at Johnny with starstruck eyes. "You're famous."

Johnny slanted a look toward Rachel and wondered what she'd heard. Judging from her wary expression, obviously the rumor mill had made its way around, including the good, the bad and the ugly. "Fame's not all it's cracked up to be," he muttered, but the kid scrunched his nose as if he didn't understand.

Rachel didn't give him time to say more. Instead, her look turned chilly. "The ad said to contact Brody Bloodworth. Is he here?"

Johnny shook his head, sensing she didn't want to talk to him. Dammit. Maybe his reputation had preceded him. It bothered him more than he wanted to think.

"Afraid not. Brody had business in town." He gestured toward a comfy leather couch facing an oak coffee table loaded with horse and ranching magazines along with brochures about the services, accommodations, camps, trail rides and other programs the BBL offered. "We're just getting set up now, so there's a million things to do. But I can get you an application."

Through the window, Kenny noticed Kim working with a quarter horse in the pen and tugged at Rachel's hand. "Can I watch the horses, Mommy?"

"Of course, buddy." Rachel squeezed his shoulder and gave him such a tender, motherly smile that something moved inside Johnny's chest.

The apprehension the little boy had had earlier seemed to dissipate slightly as he raced over and looked out the window.

When Johnny glanced back at Rachel, he had to swallow hard. Earlier, all he'd seen was a bruised and frightened woman, one who was likely running scared.

Now he realized how attractive Rachel Simmons really was, and his gut tightened. He'd sworn off women after that fiasco in Durango, and the last thing he needed to do was get tangled up with a filly in trouble. For all he knew, she might have pulled a con on some poor Joe, run off with his money, and the bruises were a sign that she'd been caught in the act.

But more likely, she'd been victimized and needed a helping hand. Wasn't that the goal of the BBL?

"What kind of job are you looking for?" he asked.

Rachel twisted her hands together. "I can do anything—cook, clean houses or cabins, work with the kids, muck stalls, groom horses."

"Have you worked on a ranch before?"

A nervous flitter entered her eyes. "Not exactly, but I've done lots of odd jobs."

"What kind of jobs?"

She sighed. "Waitressing. Dishwasher. Factory work. Cleaning. Retail sales. Receptionist—"

He held up his hand. "Okay, I get the point." She sounded educated, but all those odd jobs…

"Where are you from?"

She curled her fingers tighter inside her palms, another sign that she was trying to hide a case of nerves. Or lies.

"Here and there. We've moved around a lot."

Uh-huh. Definitely sounded like someone running from trouble.

He lowered his voice, "And the boy's father?"

She quickly glanced at her son, then back at him. "It's just the two of us."

"I see." He reached inside the desk and removed

an application for employment. "Here, fill this out and list your references. Then we'll see what we can do."

Her hand trembled as she took the application, then she cast a worried look at her son.

"I...don't have any references to offer," she said quietly. "Like I said, we haven't stayed in one place very long this last year." She drew a deep breath, making her chest rise and fall, and drawing attention to how thin she was. It looked as if she hadn't had a good meal in days. The little boy looked a little on the lean side, too.

"But I'm a hard worker and a fast learner. And..." She gestured toward the brochure. "I'd like to be a part of what you're doing here."

He clenched his jaw so hard that it ached. Those protective instincts that had kicked in earlier roared off the charts.

"All right." He made a snap decision and hoped to hell he wouldn't regret it. "You can cook?"

She nodded a little too eagerly. "I've been cooking since I was born," she said as if mirroring his earlier comment about riding.

"She makes the bestest blueberry pancakes on the planet," Kenny said as he inched back to her side.

Rachel ruffled his hair with an affectionate hand, and Johnny's reservations faded. He couldn't turn her and this little boy away. He would give her a job.

At least temporarily.

"I'm afraid the salary's not great, but we have a small cabin near the dining hall, where you and your son can stay, that's included with the job. And Kenny can also participate in the camps as a perk."

Rachel gave him such a relieved and appreciative smile that his chest clenched.

"That sounds wonderful." She hugged Kenny to her, her smile deepening to reveal dimples. "Thank you so much."

Johnny amended his earlier thought. She wasn't attractive. The woman was downright drop-dead gorgeous.

But hell, that didn't mean he trusted her.

Or that he would get close to her.

As soon as he showed her around and got her settled in a cabin, he'd run a background check and find out just exactly who she was. And if she was a criminal or dangerous, he'd send her packing.

RACHEL HOPED HER DESPERATION didn't show, but she'd read the pitch for the BBL, with its promises, wide stretches of open land and location miles and miles away from San Antonio, and realized it was a perfect hideaway for her and her son.

And the type of place Rex might never think to look for her.

Rex liked city life, fancy shows, expensive restaurants and the glitzy nightlife. He wouldn't be caught dead riding a horse, cleaning a stall or touching a cow, and had adamantly refused Kenny any kind of pet.

That had been another sign that he wasn't the man she'd thought she'd married.

Besides, she and Kenny both needed to breathe some fresh air, take a break from the city hopping they'd been doing for months, and have some semblance of a normal life.

But Kenny would start school in the fall, and then what? She supposed she could homeschool, but their life had been difficult enough. Kenny needed friends his own age. Here, there would be other children and animals and land. At least for a little while...

"I can show you around and then take you to the cabin to settle in," Johnny said.

"Thank you. I can start anytime."

"Tomorrow's good enough. We don't have kids here tonight, but in the morning a group of teens from an orphanage are coming in, and we're starting our first camps."

Rachel tried to ignore the way her stomach fluttered at the sound of his rugged voice. He sounded excited at the prospect of the children's arrival.

But she'd been fooled by Rex at the beginning, by his charm. She'd never make that mistake again.

Johnny led her and Kenny outside to his pickup truck, a big, shiny, red vehicle with a gigantic cab, backseat and a truck bed nicer than any car she'd ever owned. As he drove them across the property, he gave a running monologue describing the size of the ranch, pointing out the stables, pens, creek, river, pastures and rolling hills where they would eventually expand and add to the herd.

"We're planning to teach the kids to ride, how to groom and take care of the animals—responsibility will be part of their discipline and therapy," he clarified, "and we'll organize trail rides, camps, shows and competitions."

His enthusiasm seemed so genuine that the man intrigued her. And Kenny was staring out the window of the backseat in awe.

"We'll also teach the boys how to rope and do tricks and maybe even help on a cattle drive. But in exchange they'll have to work the ranch. Help clean stalls, mend fences, build pens, feed the animals." Johnny paused. "Hard work builds character."

Rachel nodded. Rex's theory had been that money built character.

Instead, Johnny was a hands-on guy. And he had big, broad, callused hands… Sexy hands. No wonder all the women had found Johnny Long so irresistible.

But she had to be immune.

Not that he was interested in her or ever would be.

For God's sake, she had a child and a dangerous ex. And she was certainly not his type.

No, the news had shown photo after photo of him with voluptuous young blondes and redheads who followed him on the road. Rodeo groupies whose names were Candy and Brandi with an *i,* women who didn't have dishpan hands or tired, lank hair or nails chewed down to the quick from worrying about money and a son she needed to care for and protect.

Her throat thick with emotions and exhaustion, she massaged her temple, battling an unexpected rash of tears.

"There are the bunkhouses for the campers," Johnny pointed out. "They're set up like dorms and divided into quadrants according to ages. We hired some college students as camp counselors. Hopefully, as the camp and our reputation grow, we'll have returning youth who will assume that role."

"It's impressive," Rachel said, and meant it. "But I'm surprised your investors are actually physically working with the program themselves."

Johnny shifted, looking uncomfortable. When

he parked at a long building with a wooden sign that read Dining Hall and looked up at her, pain flashed briefly across his face.

"Not all of us were born with money or had things handed to us on a silver platter." His voice held a defensive hint. "Some of us…had problems of our own. Now we want to give back."

Rachel's heart stuttered at the lost-little-boy look in his eyes as his gaze met hers. She hadn't meant to sound condescending, but she must have pushed a button.

She tried to remember what she'd read about him. Something about a woman making accusations against him.

But Kenny released a squeal of excitement, halting her thoughts, and threw open his door. "Mommy, look, there's a dog! A real dog!"

Rachel glanced at the mutt and nearly choked on a laugh. Cleo was a mixed mutt of some kind, a cross between a basset hound and a beagle and God knew what else.

Johnny's troubled look faded at her son's outburst, and he turned to Kenny with a smile. "That's Cleopatra, but we call her Cleo," Johnny said. "Come on, Kenny. She's been lonely and needs a friend."

Rachel sensed he wasn't just talking about the dog. That he had figured out more about her from their initial meeting than she'd intended to reveal.

No…that wasn't possible.

Not unless Rex had followed her or some-how discovered she'd been checking out this ranch. If he had, he could have already contacted the people here. Maybe he'd called Johnny and spouted off his book of lies.

What if he'd asked Johnny to play nice to her, to lull her into a sense of safety until Rex could show up?

Her head was churning with suspicions, her panic-voice urging her to run again, so loudly that she hadn't noticed that Johnny had helped Kenny down from the truck and they were playing with the dog.

The pathetic, bony-looking animal had sprawled on the ground and was salivating as Kenny scratched between her floppy ears.

Rachel climbed down to join them, the joy on her son's face deflating her earlier worries. She was just being paranoid. There was no way Rex could know she was here.

"Mom, Cleo and I are gonna be best friends."

She knotted her hands, ready to deny him. But Johnny stood and placed a hand on her shoulder. A gentle hand that made her look up into his eyes. Eyes that were usually flirty but eyes that looked soulful now, as if he saw too much.

The realization made her shift uncomfortably.

"Cleo was a stray I found on the side of the

road," he said quietly. "She'd been abandoned and abused. She needs someone to love her."

Tears burned Rachel's throat. He sounded so sincere.

And somehow he'd sensed the fact that her son needed stability. Peace. Normalcy.

The BBL offered all those things. The kind of comfort and home neither of them had had in a very long time.

She let him guide her toward the dining hall. They would stay, she decided.

But at the first sign of trouble, that Rex had followed them, they'd hit the road and never look back.

Chapter Three

Johnny noted the skittish gleam in Rachel's eyes but forced himself not to push for the reason. Breaking horses had taught him patience, that it took time to win an animal's trust, and he figured the same for her.

Besides, did he really want to know about her problems?

No. He couldn't get caught up in her life. He was here to help the lost kids, not become involved with a woman.

But the sight of Kenny's excited face as Cleo licked his hand stirred emotions deep inside him. And so did Rachel's obvious love for her son.

Unlike his own mother...

Don't go there, Johnny.

"Let's step inside the dining hall and I'll introduce you to Ms. Ellen. She'll be the main cook and is the head honcho in the kitchen."

"Can I stay out here and play with Cleo?" Kenny asked.

Rachel glanced around the property, then chewed on her bottom lip as if debating whether she should leave him alone.

"It's okay," Johnny assured her. "It's safe here, Rachel."

Her gaze jerked to his, and for a brief second fear registered. That and distrust.

Did she think he would hurt her?

Maybe she had seen that news story...

But she conducted another visual sweep of the area, then gave a reluctant nod to her son. "Okay, Kenny, but stay here by the building. Don't wander off."

Kenny plunked down on the grass under a Texas red oak, and Cleo rested her head in his lap. "Then we can see the puppies?"

Johnny nodded. "Do as your mama says and yes, then we'll see Cleo's pups."

Kenny's crooked teeth shone as he bobbed his head up and down, then he cuddled the dog and began to rub her belly.

"He's always wanted a pet," Rachel confessed as they climbed the porch steps and entered the cafeteria-style room. "But I hope he doesn't become too attached."

Meaning she probably didn't plan on sticking around. "We'll probably be looking for homes for the pups," Johnny said anyway.

She glanced at him, but again that wary expression returned. But she was saved from answering by Ms. Ellen, who came bounding around the corner of the kitchen.

The scent of homemade cinnamon rolls filled the air, and Johnny's stomach growled.

"Well, if it ain't *the* Johnny Long," Ms. Ellen said. "You must have smelled the buns in the oven."

"Thought I was smelling heaven," Johnny said with a wink. Ms. Ellen was a plump middle-aged woman with a smile as broad as her hips and a heart that never quit giving. When Brody had mentioned needing a cook, Johnny had visited one of the homeless shelters near San Antonio and found the gem of a woman.

After all, she needed a second chance herself, so hiring her was the perfect solution.

Ms. Ellen wiped her hands on her apron and looked at Rachel. "And who is this, Mr. J.? Your girlfriend?"

Rachel's face blanched, and Johnny nearly choked. "No...uh...she's your new assistant cook."

"Well, thank the Lord," Ms. Ellen said. "With all those hungry kids and the hands coming in, I need some help." She narrowed her eyes. "But you're awfully skinny, girl. You really know how to cook?"

Rachel smiled, seemingly grateful to have the awkward moment pass. "Yes, ma'am."

Ms. Ellen made a smacking sound with her mouth. "Well, then, welcome to Ms. Ellen's kitchen. How about I show you around?"

"Can it wait till tomorrow?" Johnny said. "She just arrived, so I need to give her a tour of the rest of the ranch and settle her into a cabin."

Ms. Ellen nodded, then bundled up them both some cinnamon rolls before she allowed them to leave. Johnny dug into one as they walked back outside, then handed one to Kenny, whose face lit up as he sank his teeth into the gooey pastry.

Rachel laughed, and the three of them, plus Cleo, climbed back into his truck for the rest of the tour. He showed her the stables where they kept the quarter horses, the pens for training and for riding lessons, the arena where they planned to hold the rodeo, and the barn and pastures for the beef cattle and calves.

Kenny seemed to loosen up, his excitement mounting with each discovery, and Rachel finally relaxed. And when Johnny showed them inside the barn, and Kenny saw the puppies, he thought he detected tears in Rachel's eyes.

"Kenny," Johnny said gruffly. "If you're going to stay here, you have to earn your keep."

Kenny's smile faded and apprehension streaked his little face. Then he inched closer to his mother and ducked behind her, his big eyes frightened again. "Yes, sir."

Johnny grimaced at the sudden change in the boy's demeanor.

"What does he have to do?" Rachel asked, her tone defensive.

Johnny knelt in front of Kenny and scooped up one of the puppies. "I thought you'd look after Cleo and her boys. Make sure Cleo gets food and water every day, and play with the pups. They're just babies and need exercise."

The frightened expression in Kenny's eyes morphed from relief to childlike glee in a millisecond.

"Do you think you can do that for me?" Johnny asked, careful to use a gentle voice. "It would really help me out."

"Yes, sir, I can do it." Kenny squared his shoulders as if he was a little man and had just been given an important job.

Johnny gave him a high five, but the boy's reaction still troubled him. Kenny had expected something worse to be asked of him. Just what had happened to the kid?

Johnny glanced at Rachel and noticed she was trembling slightly.

Dammit. He hadn't meant to frighten her or the boy. But someone else obviously had. And he intended to find out who it was.

Then he'd see to it that it never happened again.

RACHEL SAVORED THE FRESH night air as Johnny showed them to the cabin, yet her eyes constantly scanned the area for signs that Rex had followed them.

"The cabin isn't large," Johnny said almost apologetically. "But it's clean and furnished and you'll have your own kitchen, so you can make meals on your days off and if you and Kenny decide not to eat every meal in the dining hall."

He unlocked the door and Kenny bounded in, racing through the den/kitchen combination to explore.

"There are two bedrooms," Johnny said. "But you'll share a bath."

"That's fine," Rachel said, admiring the wood floors and beams in the ceiling. "This has a lot of rustic charm." And was more cozy and homey, with its country furnishings, throw rugs, pillows and the painting of horses above the couch, than any place she'd stayed in the past year.

"Mom, there's bunk beds!" Kenny shouted from the second bedroom.

Johnny chuckled. "I always wanted bunks when I was a kid."

"Did you get them?" Rachel asked, curious about the rodeo star. He'd seemed so...normal today. Not like the arrogant playboy the papers had claimed him to be.

He shook his head. "Nope. A couple of friends

of mine, we built a fort in an old tree. That was about as close as I got." A faint blush stained his cheeks. "But I did put them in one of my guest rooms at my place."

Rachel quirked a brow, wondering about that detail. Had he planned to have a family someday?

He shifted, then gripped the front door. "Let me help you bring your stuff in, then I'll let you get settled."

"I can handle it," Rachel said, stiffening.

Kenny raced back in. "I can see the horses from the window by the top bunk."

Rachel smiled. It had been a long time since she'd seen her son so happy.

She only wished it could last.

"Come on, partner," Johnny said to Kenny. "Let's bring in your stuff."

Kenny loped up beside Johnny and the two of them headed back to her Jeep. Rachel followed, tensing as Johnny opened the back and spotted the two small suitcases.

He pivoted to look at her, questions in his eyes. "Is this it?"

She nodded. "We like to travel light." *Because I had to leave my other stuff behind.*

He stared at her for a long minute, then nodded, lifted her suitcase and Kenny's smaller one, handed Kenny his backpack of toys and strode back inside the cabin.

Rachel heard a truck rumble and jerked around, fighting panic, her heart racing as she searched for Rex.

But the truck rolled on past in a cloud of dust.

She sighed in relief, grateful for the reprieve as she met Johnny on the steps.

She just wondered how long it would last.

REX SLID LOWER INTO THE seat of his car, where he'd parked beneath a cluster of live oaks, his fingers sliding over the Smith & Wesson in his hands as he studied the Georgian house with the gigantic columns and sculpted shrubs.

The house belonged to Judge Walton Hammers. A rich, powerful man who held the fate of people's lives in his hands.

An arrogant bastard who'd signed the papers granting Rachel the divorce.

A chuckle rumbled deep in his chest. The stupid, fat fool had no idea that by doing so he'd signed his own death warrant.

A Mercedes rolled up and Rex tensed, his heart pounding, his fingers itching to do the job. The judge steered the Mercedes into the driveway, then hit the garage door opener, and the door slid up. The Mercedes coasted inside, then the lights flicked off.

Night had fallen, dark shadows casting the mansion in gray as Rex climbed from the sedan, grabbed his rope and inched his way along the wooded lot toward the garage.

He tiptoed into the space, hiding in the shadows as the judge and his wife climbed from the car. The judge staggered, a little tipsy, and his wife moved around to help him inside.

Rex gripped his gun at the ready, then bolted up behind them and jammed the gun at the judge's back.

"Inside now. And disarm the security."

The woman shrieked and the judge started to turn around, but Rex crammed the gun in his back. "Do it or you both die."

"Who the hell are you?" the judge grumbled.

"Just do as he s-says," his wife cried.

The judge stumbled in, his wife gripping his arm, and punched the alarm. Rex relaxed slightly at the sound of the beep, then shoved the man into the room.

"Why are you doing this?" the judge bellowed.

The wife started to sob. "Please, my jewelry is upstairs. Just take what you want and don't hurt us!"

Rex released a sinister laugh. Good idea. Make it look like a robbery gone bad.

"Up the steps," he ordered.

The judge tilted his head sideways to look at him, but Rex jerked his arm. "I told you to move!"

"You won't get away with this," the judge growled.

Rex shoved them both toward the hallway and followed them as they climbed the winding staircase, the wife clutching her husband as if she might fall if he didn't hold her up. When they entered the bedroom, the judge reached for a light.

"No." Rex shoved the woman onto the bed, jammed the gun at the judge's head, then pushed the rope into his hands. "Tie her up."

The judge stammered a protest, but Rex turned the gun on his wife and he complied. The woman cried and wept as her husband bound her hands and feet, and the judge kept apologizing to her, promising that it would be all right. When he had the knots secure, Rex ordered the judge to sit down beside her.

"Just take the jewelry, and there's money in my safe," the judge offered in a shaky voice. "You can have it all. Just don't hurt my wife."

Rex barked a laugh. "You don't understand, Judge. You took my wife from me. Now I want you to feel that same pain."

With a flick of his finger, he pulled the trigger and shot the woman in the head. She screamed a second before the bullet pierced her brain. Blood splattered, then she slumped onto the bed in a flood of red.

The judge bellowed in shock and grief, then charged toward him. Rex pulled the trigger, firing a round into the fat man's gut.

Then he pushed him back onto the bed and sat down, smiling as the blood began to seep from the judge's belly.

The judge groaned and wheezed for a breath, struggling to get back up and fight.

But it was useless. He was going to die. It was only a matter of time.

The sweet taste of victory surged through him, and he fired a shot into the man's kneecap and was rewarded by a loud scream of pain.

The woman's death had been quick and relatively painless.

But the judge would die slowly, bleeding to death.

He grinned. He would watch the old bastard suffer until the end.

Chapter Four

The next few days Rachel avoided Johnny as much as possible. He was nice to her, good with Kenny and patient with the older boys who'd arrived. He had allowed Kenny to join in the camp activities with the other children, and let her son follow him around. He tolerated his questions and never lost his temper.

He was too good to be true.

And too sexy.

Not that she was interested in sex. No, Rex had ruined that for her, too.

But as she hurried back to the dining hall to help Ms. Ellen with dinner, she spotted him working with a group of teens in one of the pens. He was teaching them how to rope a calf, his muscles bunching as he gripped the animal and tied the rope around its legs.

She kept waiting for the ball to drop, for him to go off on one of the boys like Rex would have, but so far, he'd remained calm and in control.

Was the article she'd read about him having a hot temper simply gossip?

Kenny hung on to the fence, watching, infatuated with the cowboy's every move.

Apprehension tightened her shoulders. If he grew too fond of the man, it would only make it more difficult when they had to leave.

And she had no doubt that that moment would come.

Rex's harsh words echoed in her ears. *I'll kill you next time.*

He would never give up. He would find them. And then the running would have to start again. A new name. A new town.

A new house or apartment or trailer, whatever she could find.

Another reason she couldn't call the little cabin she and Kenny were staying in home. Although, the fireplace and homemade quilts and warm earthy tones made it cozy, and it felt more like home than any place she'd ever lived.

So did the dining hall. And Ms. Ellen... She was like a grandmother to Kenny and a second mom to her.

She liked Kim, Johnny's sister, too, and her four-year-old little girl, Lucy, was adorable.

Kim taught riding skills to the younger campers and also did personal counseling, and Lucy and Kenny had enjoyed playing together.

Ranch life started early and she rose at five-thirty to help with the day's meals while Kenny fed Cleo and played with the pups. Ms. Ellen arrived at the kitchen at four to start breakfast, but she always greeted her and Kenny with a warm smile and a pan of hot biscuits or cinnamon buns.

It was the first time since her parents died that she'd come close to having a semblance of a family.

She was desperately afraid she and Kenny were both losing their hearts to the ranch and the people here.

"Come on, Rachel," Ms. Ellen called. "This barbecue sauce needs your special touch."

Rachel grinned and went to taste the sauce, then added a dollop of molasses, and Ellen deemed it perfect. For the next two hours, they worked side by side, setting up the buns and Brunswick stew and slicing brownies to add to the dessert table along with bowls of homemade banana pudding.

A group of young boys from a middle school in a lower-income area filed in, then another church group of day-trippers, then six teenage boys from the orphanage. Two of the older boys looked rough around the edges, with tattoos and scowls that indicated a bad attitude. Rachel tensed as the oldest one, Ricardo, glared at her from the food line.

"This is pig slop," the boy muttered.

Suddenly, Johnny appeared beside him. "Treat

the lady with respect," Johnny said in a tone that brooked no argument. "And if you don't like the food, you can do without."

Ricardo looked up at Johnny, his face turning to stone, but he nodded and mumbled an apology. Still, something about the sinister gleam in his eyes suggested he was faking it in front of Johnny. That if Johnny wasn't around, he'd let his true side shine, just like Rex.

A shiver rippled up Rachel's spine, but Kenny loped up, wearing a black Stetson like Johnny's and imitating Johnny's stance, and thoughts of the other boy fled.

"Look at my hat, Mom!" Kenny tipped the Stetson to show off the silver trim around the brim. "It's just like Mr. J.'s!"

Rachel's heart clenched at the hero worship in her young son's eyes. "It's awesome," Rachel said tightly, but she frowned at Johnny as she handed him a plate.

His gaze met hers, and his brow furrowed in question, but then one of the middle school boys called his name and he turned to talk to them.

"Tell us about the time you won that big trophy for penning," one of the boys said.

Johnny joined the boys at the table, then began to entertain them with his rodeo stories.

"I wanna learn to ride like that," a ten-year-old named Pedro said.

"Me, too," another boy yelled. "And I wanna learn to pen just like you, Mr. J.!"

Kenny piped up. "Can I be in the rodeo?"

Johnny patted Kenny's shoulder. "Sure. We'll start working on some riding skills tomorrow." He fisted his hand and placed it in the middle of the table. "Who's in?"

The boys clamored with excitement, balling their hands into fists and stacking them on top of Johnny's until he gave the signal and they all shouted a cheer.

"He's so good with the children," Ms. Ellen commented. "Your little one seems to have taken a shine to him."

"Yes, I see," Rachel said, although her stomach was twisted in knots.

"Where is his papa?" Ms. Ellen asked.

Rachel added more buns and barbecue on the trays for the ranch hands filing in. "It's just me and Kenny."

"Then Mr. J. is a good role model, right?"

Rachel chewed her bottom lip. "Yes, it looks that way." But she hurried to finish restocking the remainder of the food trays, determined to avoid the subject. One thing she'd learned on the run was to avoid intimacy with anyone.

Even well-meaning people like Ms. Ellen, because Rex might hurt the woman to get to her.

The next two hours flew by as she and Ms.

Ellen served the ranch hands, grooms, camp counselors and other staff. So far, she'd yet to meet Brody, but Ms. Ellen assured her he was a fine man with a good heart.

Kenny hung with the other boys until she and Ms. Ellen had cleaned up and she was ready to leave. As she and Kenny stepped outside, she breathed in the fresh air, savoring the scent of fresh grass and the hint of wildflowers in the air.

But gravel crunched and she jerked around, immediately on edge.

Johnny hesitated, narrowing his eyes. "Sorry, I didn't mean to startle you. I just thought I'd walk you two back to your cabin."

Hating to be caught off guard, Rachel stiffened. "We're fine on our own."

Johnny shrugged but fell in beside her anyway, his sexy swagger irritating her to no end. Heaven help her. She didn't want to like him, but from what she'd seen, he was great with the kids. And he was so tough and masculine at the same time that he was downright irresistible.

But she had to resist. Besides, he might be wearing a mask to fool her just like Rex had.

Kenny broke into a run as they neared the cabin.

"I'm gonna see Cleo and the pups!"

The barn door banged shut as Kenny rushed inside, and Johnny turned to her, concern etched on his chiseled face. "Kenny seemed nervous when you first got here, but he's starting to open up."

Rachel tensed. She didn't intend to answer questions about her past.

Even more unsettling was Johnny's masculine presence. And the scent of his body was so intoxicating that she could hardly breathe. What was it? Some woodsy smell and sweat? It shouldn't be so potent or inviting, but for some reason, it stirred desires she'd thought crushed to death by Rex's brute force.

"What's wrong, Rachel?" Johnny asked. "Why was Kenny so scared when you first arrived?"

"He's just shy around new people." Her defenses rose and she whirled toward him. "Why did you give Kenny that hat like yours?"

He narrowed his eyes in confusion. "He liked mine so much I thought he'd enjoy having one of his own. Is something wrong?"

No, it really was very nice. Touching even. But neither of them could get accustomed to it. "I appreciate you being kind to him, but you can't give him gifts without asking me first."

"I'm sorry," Johnny said. "I didn't mean to offend you."

Rachel recognized the sincerity in his voice and felt like a heel. "It's just that he can't get used to receiving gifts from you or anyone else. Especially things that I can't give him."

He gave her a devilish smile, a leftover of his rodeo days. "It's just a hat, Rachel, nothing more."

Rachel's mouth thinned. "I don't want him hanging false hopes about staying here or…"

"Or what?" Johnny asked.

Rachel didn't know how to explain her reaction without revealing the truth. And the truth could be dangerous for them all.

"I just don't want him to become too attached," she finally admitted.

"Because you don't plan to stay?"

God help her, she wanted to stay. She was tired of running, but what choice did she have?

"I…don't know," she said quietly. "I just don't want Kenny to get hurt."

Johnny folded his arms. "I would never hurt your son or any of these boys."

Rachel believed he wouldn't intentionally harm him. But allowing Kenny to idolize him then to be torn away from him one day could crush her son.

She started to turn away, but Johnny caught her arm. "Rachel, tell me what's wrong. Let me be your friend."

The moment his fingers closed around her wrist, a shudder coursed through her as unbidden memories of Rex nearly snapping her wrist in two as she'd tried to walk away from him crashed back.

"I don't need a friend. I can take care of myself and my son." She jerked her arm away, then rubbed at her wrist and stepped toward the barn to get Kenny.

"Everyone needs a friend," Johnny said in a gruff voice.

Rachel shook her head, unable to voice the fears gnawing at her. She couldn't share the truth, couldn't let him or anyone into their lives. If Rex saw her with Johnny, even if nothing personal was going on between them, he'd go out of his mind with jealousy. He'd done it before.

He might even attack Johnny before he killed her.

And just like before, the police wouldn't believe her. Not with Rex's connections.

So she turned and ran inside the house. She'd call Kenny in a minute. But first she needed a moment to calm her raging emotions.

Maybe she should leave the BBL tonight. Johnny was already suspicious. He might have already run a background check. If not, and if he decided to look into her past and discovered the warrant for her arrest, he might turn her in to the sheriff.

Then she'd go to jail and her son would never have a chance.

But the moment she entered the cabin, she froze, her lungs choking as the scent of another man's cologne wafted toward her. Not Johnny's woodsy scent, but an expensive brand that nauseated her because it reminded her of Rex.

Dear God, had he found her?

JOHNNY WANTED TO ASSURE Rachel he was only trying to be nice to her son. But he couldn't force her into liking him or sharing her past.

Dammit. He'd put off checking into her background. Why, he didn't know.

Maybe because she was so damn pretty and looked so lost and frightened and in need of a friend. Or maybe it had to do with her son. Maybe Kenny reminded him of himself at that age.

But he couldn't stall running the background check any longer. Not with the other kids around.

He walked back to the dining hall, retrieved his truck, then drove back to the main headquarters. Inside, he grabbed a cold beer, then slipped inside the office. He hated to probe, but he was her employer and they had rules, so he phoned the service they used to run background checks.

Troy Staley, the guy the BBL had used before, answered and plugged Rachel's name into the database.

He took a long pull from the bottle and waited several seconds, then Troy spoke.

"Several different women with that name popped up, Johnny. The first is seventy-five and lives in Wyoming."

"So it's a common name," Johnny said, although his pulse was clamoring.

"Yeah. There's also a teenager from Georgia who won a beauty pageant." Troy sighed. "I'm checking down the list, but none of them match the description you gave me. Well, except the last one. But that Rachel Simmons was buried in Austin three weeks ago."

Hmm, she'd lived in Texas and was about the same age as Rachel.

He frowned, his mind clicking away various possibilities. Maybe the database had missed her for some reason.

Or maybe Rachel had given him a fake name. But why?

"Thanks, man. If you find out anything else, give me a call."

"Right, I'll keep looking."

Johnny disconnected, then headed out the door, irritated that Rachel might have placed the kids at the BBL in danger. Night had fallen, the full moon a ball of fire casting a shimmering glow across the pastures as he climbed into his truck and drove to her cabin.

He loved his own spread, but this place had come to life with the kids this week. And for the first time in years, he felt as if he was doing something worthwhile.

He couldn't let anyone jeopardize the operation or the people here.

The truck rumbled across the dirt drive, the sight of the quarter horses they'd just brought in running through the east pasture a reminder that he had to start organizing the rodeo. Plan the events, advertise, make posters... It was going to take time and all his focus.

A vehicle parked at the ridge by the creek on the hill drew his eye, and he frowned. Maybe one of the grooms or ranch hands had driven out there for some fresh air? He craned his neck to see the make of the vehicle, but didn't recognize it.

Odd.

Still, he didn't know every SUV or truck belonging to the hands.

Then again, what if their neighbor Rich Copeland was snooping around? He'd protested when Brody had bought the land and designated it for a kids' camp. Copeland tried to stir up supporters to stop Brody, claiming troubled boys would endanger his own property and hands. Brody had tried to make the man understand that his fears were unfounded, but Copeland wouldn't back down and had spread rumors and stirred animosity and worry with others in town. There was bad blood between the men now.

He'd reached Rachel's cabin and forgot about the vehicle and Copeland as he pulled to a stop and tried to determine the best way to approach her.

Sucking in a sharp breath, he climbed out, pausing to study the cabin. Even though she'd been here only a few days, Rachel had planted flowers in the flower boxes and had attached wind chimes from the awning of the front porch. She'd even hung the bird feeder Kenny had built in the day camp with the other boys and filled it with birdseed.

As if she was making this a home.

Guilt slammed into his gut for what he was about to do. Because if she didn't come clean with him, he had no choice. He'd have to ask her to leave.

And that meant tearing out a little boy's heart.

No wonder she hadn't wanted Kenny getting attached to him.

He started toward the porch, but suddenly a scream pierced the air. A woman's scream… Rachel…

The image of her bruises flashed in his mind, and he took off running.

KENNY THOUGHT HE HEARD a scream outside. He clutched the butterball puppy to him and craned his head to hear again.

No, it had to be the wind. He was safe and so was his mama.

He stretched against a haystack, and Cleo plopped her head in his lap. The puppies started crawling all over him, up his leg, and the fat one fell off and rolled onto its back with a squeal.

Kenny rubbed its belly, then helped it turn over. The fat butterball got on his feet but wobbled and fell over again and he laughed.

Cleo snuggled against his arm and he hugged the dog.

"I like it here, Cleo," he said, nuzzling her neck. "And I really like Mr. J."

The dog licked his neck, and he swallowed back tears. He was a big boy and not supposed to cry.

But his mama was scared. She jumped at every little sound. He just knew any minute she'd tell him it was time to leave.

"I don't wanna leave," he whispered to Cleo.

But a shadow moved in the barn, and just like his mama, he jumped. A squeaking sound came from the far corner, and he scooted back behind the haystack, pulling the puppies with him. The butterball one got away, though, and waddled across the barn floor.

Kenny held his breath.

Had his daddy found them? Was he in the barn?

He choked back a cry. If he was, he might hurt the puppy.

Kenny looked around for something to fend him off with if he came toward him. A stick or a rock. Anything to save the little butterball from his daddy.

Outside he heard a scream.

Not the wind. His mama.

His heart pounded. He had to save her. "I love you, Cleo," Kenny whispered. He hugged the dog, then scratched behind her floppy ears and settled Cleo back down beside the other puppies.

The butterball one had made it to the door, and he ran to get her, then carried her back and put her in the stall. His legs felt shaky, and he wanted to hide inside the barn with the dogs.

But he remembered the bruises on his mama's face and neck, and he balled his hands into fists. Then he ran back to the barn door and peered outside.

Daddies were supposed to be nice like Mr. J.

But his daddy was a monster.

He couldn't let him hurt his mama anymore. He just wished he was big and strong like Mr. J. so he could stop him.

He sucked in a big breath and slowly opened the door. He might not be big and strong, but he'd try anyway.

Chapter Five

Rachel stared at the snake lying in the middle of her bed with revulsion. Her first instinct was to run.

But running might make the snake strike.

Suddenly the door screeched open, and she heard Johnny's gruff voice. "Rachel?"

In spite of the fact that she was desperately trying not to move, a tremor rippled through her and her legs wobbled.

His boots pounded on the floor as he crossed the room coming closer. "Rachel?"

She had to clear her throat to make her voice work. "In here."

His footsteps grew louder, then she glanced sideways and saw him at the doorway, his pistol drawn. He quickly glanced around, his expression worried.

"What's wrong? I heard you scream."

"There. The bed…" Rachel pointed to the

snake. It was almost two feet long, with red-and-black coloring. "Is...it poisonous?"

Johnny muttered a sound of frustration, then inched into the room and lowered his gun. "How the hell did that get in here?"

"I don't know." Rachel fought a surge of tears. She had an idea, but she couldn't tell him or he'd know the truth about her. That Kenny's father was not only alive but a terrifying, cruel man who liked to torment her.

That her worst fear might have come true. That Rex had found her and was trying to scare her.

That putting a snake in the bed, sneaking inside her room and messing with her things, leaving mysterious presents, torn photos of her and Kenny, one of Kenny's stuffed animals ripped and shredded, a dead rat, a black rose...they were all things he'd done before.

Things his warped sense of humor and twisted sense of love found funny. Things he hoped would frighten her back into his arms and make her give him back his son.

He was sick, demented, a psychopath.

She would never go back to him or let him near Kenny.

The mere thought that he'd been in the room made her ill, and a strangled sound gurgled in her throat.

Johnny closed his hand around her arm to

steady her. "It's okay. It looks like a coral snake and they are poisonous, but this is a milk snake."

She was shaking so badly that she swayed, and Johnny pulled her up against him and closed his arms around her. She leaned into him for just a moment and took a deep breath, but his masculine scent made her dizzy in another way, and she pulled away. "How can you tell the difference?"

He spoke in a calm voice. "The coral snake's red and yellow colors touch, but the milk snake has red touching black and is harmless."

She chanced a look at him and saw that he was watching her with worried eyes. He was such a pillar of strength that she wanted to fall into his arms. But she couldn't trust him or any other man.

"They still bite, don't they?"

"Snakes strike back as a defensive mechanism." Johnny moved slowly toward the bed, careful not to make a sudden noise and startle the snake.

"I don't care. I don't want him in my bed."

"Don't worry," Johnny said. "We'll take care of that."

His voice remained low, his footfalls light until he reached the bed, then he lifted the snake with his hands, carefully holding its mouth away from him, and crossed the room. Shivering, she followed him outside.

Kenny came running up then, with Cleo trailing him. His eyes widened when he spotted Johnny with the snake. Then his gaze flew to her, and Rachel realized he'd heard her scream and had thought Rex had found them.

Guilt slammed into her. Her poor little boy. He shouldn't have to be afraid of his own father. "It's okay, Kenny. A snake was in the house. You know your mother doesn't like reptiles."

Kenny's terrified look turned to childlike curiosity, proving he was resilient.

Johnny knelt to show Kenny the snake. "It's a milk snake and harmless," Johnny explained. "But there are other snakes on the ranch that are dangerous, Kenny. Rattlers, cottonmouths, copperheads. You need to be careful when you're out in the field, or if you're by the river or creek." He paused. "The counselors will teach you how to recognize the poisonous ones. Be careful when you pick up a stick or turn over a rock or log."

Kenny nodded, soaking in every word Johnny spoke. "Can I pet him?" Kenny asked, wide-eyed.

"Sure, but you need to run your finger down his body. If you rub against his scales, it'll hurt him."

Rachel clenched her hands as she watched the gentle way Johnny handled the reptile and her son. But the scent of that cologne in her cabin and the fact that she had found the snake in her bed made her chest clench with fear.

Kenny really liked it on the ranch.

But if Rex was here, they would have to leave Cleo and the pups and his new friend and idol Johnny behind.

SUSPICIONS REARED THEMSELVES in Johnny's head, making his temper come alive, but he bit his tongue to keep from voicing them aloud.

Rachel was definitely lying to him. About her name. About the reason she had been traveling from town to town. Maybe about everything else.

Something had her spooked, bad, and it wasn't just that damn snake.

Which raised suspicion number two. How the hell had it gotten in her bed? Sure, they found snakes in the barn and on the ranch, but so far they hadn't managed to worm their way inside any of the cabins. And if Rachel had locked the cabin up when she'd left and the windows were shut…

"What are you gonna do with him?" Kenny asked.

"Let him go." Johnny frowned, then stood. "You see, Kenny, farms and ranches need snakes to eat smaller rodents. It's God's way of balancing nature."

Rachel watched him, her arms folded around her waist as if she was trying to hold herself together. Some people had an aversion to snakes, but her reaction seemed over-the-top.

Kenny tugged at his shirt. "Can I help you let him go?"

Johnny looked up at Rachel. "Sure, buddy. Then I'll check the cabin to make sure it's clean."

The wary look that flickered in Rachel's eyes made him wish he could retract his statement.

He wanted a moment alone with her.

Maybe to pull her into his arms again?

Watch out, Johnny. This woman is trouble.

And you have a ranch and a bunch of children to protect.

Relief softened her face. "Thank you. I'll sleep better if I'm certain there are no more predators inside."

Her word choice struck him as odd but telling.

Just what kind of predator was after Rachel and her son?

Kenny tagged along beside him as they walked to the pasture to release the snake.

"My mom don't like bugs or spiders, either," Kenny said, jerking Johnny from his thoughts.

Johnny smiled at the boy. "Most girls don't, bud."

Kenny squared his little shoulders. "Yeah, but us guys, we gots to protect the girls. That's what real men do."

Real men? "What do you have to protect your mom from?"

Kenny angled his face toward the dirt as if he'd

said something he shouldn't, and Johnny's heart ached. He sensed the kid wanted to tell him more.

"Kenny?" Johnny said softly. "I'm your friend, and your mother's friend. If you need someone to talk to, you can talk to me."

The little boy looked up at him with such a grown-up expression that Johnny wanted to take the weight of the world off his small shoulders.

But Kenny simply shrugged. "Thanks, but me and Mama, we take care of each other."

Johnny's chest constricted. God, he understood how the kid felt. When his mama had left and his daddy had gone on his drunken raging tears, he had taken care of Kim.

And they had kept the beatings a secret.

He hated to think that Kenny and Rachel were dealing with the same kind of monster he and Kim had lived with. And that they suffered the same shame.

Shame they didn't deserve.

"Looking forward to your riding lesson tomorrow?" he asked as they headed back toward the cabin.

"Yes, sir." Kenny's face brightened, excitement replacing the earlier fear.

The boy's hesitation once again reminded him of his own sorry childhood, and he wanted to sweep Kenny in his arms and promise him he'd never have to worry again.

But first he'd have to figure out who had the kid and his mother so spooked.

Then he'd get rid of the problem so that Kenny and Rachel would never have to be afraid or run again.

RACHEL WATCHED JOHNNY search the cabin, beneath the bed, in corners, the closet, and inside the bathroom and kitchen cabinets.

"No more snakes," he said, glancing at the bed where Rachel had stripped the covers and replaced the sheets with fresh ones from the linen closet.

"I don't know how it got in. Maybe a door was left open."

"Not by me," Rachel said. She was fanatical about checking locks and doors and windows.

Johnny shrugged as if he had no answer, but she'd already kept him long enough and was beginning to feel like a fool for overreacting.

Damn Rex for making her so paranoid that she was behaving like a crazy woman.

Kenny had crawled along beside Johnny, searching each corner and crevice with him and mimicking every movement Johnny made. Now they stood side by side, Kenny trying to look big and tough like the cowboy he admired.

Like the one she was beginning to admire, as well.

A big mistake.

She squared her shoulders. "Thank you for checking," Rachel said. "I didn't mean to get hysterical."

A smile quirked at the corner of his mouth, making him look even more handsome, and he tipped his hat. "No problem, ma'am." He patted Kenny's back. "Thanks for helping me, Kenny. Now you'd best go to bed. We start early tomorrow."

Kenny grinned and ran to give Rachel a hug. "Mr. J.'s going to teach me to ride. And I'm gonna help him make posters for the rodeo."

"We have a lot to do to prepare for the big day," Johnny said, then watched Kenny run to his bedroom.

Rachel's heart swelled at the excitement in her son's face. And when she looked back at Johnny, a flutter of sexual awareness rippled between them. He'd been kind to her son and to her.

He was nothing like Rex....

It didn't matter. Her life was too complicated for any kind of relationship with a man. Even a friendship.

"Is there anything else you need before I leave?" Johnny asked.

Rachel clenched her hands together. Yes, she wanted him to hold her. To remind her that men could be kind and loving. To purge the memory of Rex's vile touches from her mind.

But that was impossible. So she shook her head. "I'm fine, just really tired. Like you said, we start early tomorrow."

Johnny's eyes seemed to bore into hers as if he wanted to say more. As if he knew she was holding something back.

But he didn't ask. Instead, he walked out the door with a husky good-night.

For a brief second, Rachel considered running after him. Pouring out her heart and confiding about Rex. Begging him for his help.

But admitting that she had married a man like Rex meant revealing she'd been a fool. It meant reliving the shame she'd experienced in her marriage.

And confessing the truth might endanger Johnny.

She couldn't live with herself if Rex hurt him to get to her. Not after he'd been so nice to Kenny.

She hurried to tuck Kenny into bed, but he was already asleep. The fresh air, outdoor activity and chores had been good for him. He was thriving on the BBL.

She stroked a lock of his dark hair away from his forehead, then dropped a kiss on his forehead and tiptoed from the room.

Exhausted, she pulled on a nightshirt, then

crawled beneath the covers. Surely she had imagined the odor of Rex's cologne earlier.

But when she closed her eyes, she saw his face as if he was hovering above her. And for the millionth time she tried to figure out how she'd made such a mistake in marrying him.

He'd seemed so charming and handsome when they'd first met in Alabama. She'd lost her parents as a teenager and had struggled over their death and the grief and loneliness that had followed. She'd worked as a waitress at a local bar to pay her way through college.

But her junior year, Rex had walked in, ordered a scotch, then turned on the charm. The promises and gifts that followed had snowed her into a whirlwind romance. Rex had money, power and connections. He was a prominent businessman, had political connections, was going places and promised she'd go with him.

So she'd quit school and married him.

The first year of marriage had been filled with romantic getaways, sex, surprises and cocktail parties where she met all the movers and shakers in his business world.

But then she'd gotten pregnant and he'd become irate. He'd accused her of doing it on purpose. A child would interfere with his life, his plans.

She'd promised it wouldn't.

So he'd settled down for a while, but slowly his temper had edged its way into their daily lives. He was obsessed with cleanliness, with appearances and being in control.

Then one night she'd forgotten to arrange for a babysitter and had missed one of his parties. He'd been furious. Had had too much to drink. Had shouted that he'd married her to show her off. That she had promised a child wouldn't change anything.

But it had changed everything for her.

And so had his erratic mood swings.

Of course, no one else ever saw that dark side. He was like Dr. Jekyll and Mr. Hyde. A charmer on the exterior, a showman.

An evil stranger at home.

She couldn't raise her son with a controlling, abusive man, so she'd asked for a divorce.

She shuddered, a panic attack threatening as the chilling memory washed over her.

Nausea rose in her throat, and she sat up in bed and took several deep breaths to calm herself. Darkness bathed the room and, for a moment, she thought a shadow moved in the corner.

Her heart started drumming, and she flipped on the lamp, then peered around the room. Thankfully, it was empty.

Still, she was trembling, so she checked to make sure her gun was locked in the box in the closet, then brought the box and hid it between the bed and the wall. Then she tucked the key beneath her pillow.

Finally, she crawled back in bed, but sleep eluded her.

The scent of that cologne haunted her. Had Rex been in the cabin?

Finally, unable to sleep, she retrieved the key to her gun case from beneath the pillow and clutched it in her hand. If Rex was here and broke in, she'd be ready.

And if he tried to hurt her or take Kenny, she wouldn't hesitate—she'd kill him.

FROM HIS PERCH ON THE HILL, Rex watched the cabin where Rachel—or whatever the hell name she'd assumed this time—and his son slept.

The money he'd paid to find her was worth it. She'd be shocked at how easy it had been.

But he wouldn't let her know he was here yet.

A smile curved his mouth. No, he'd toy with her first. Watch her squirm. Worry. Torment her with reminders of his love.

And that he would never let her go.

If she fought him, he'd end it once and for all.

Then he'd take Kenny and hightail it to Mexico, where he could live the good life. Away from anyone who might come after him.

The lights flicked off and he smiled, picturing Rachel undressing, naked, lying in bed.

She had been a bad girl by breaking her vows and stealing his son from him. A very bad girl.

And bad girls had to be punished.

Chapter Six

Johnny barely slept for thinking about Rachel and Kenny. Their situation triggered the recurring nightmares he'd suffered for years.

The beatings his old man had given him. The drunken rages where he'd broken furniture over Johnny's head. Where he'd driven the car into the middle of the shack and caused it to set fire.

The time he'd come after Kim.

Johnny had grabbed a knife that time and stabbed his old man in the leg. That had earned him a broken arm and nose, several busted ribs, plus scars that he still had today. Scars and three weeks of barely having food.

Kim had tried to sneak him meals, but their father had caught her and thrown her against the wall. After that, Johnny had made her promise not to do anything to upset their old man.

Johnny had also vowed he'd kill the son of a bitch if he ever laid a hand on Kim again. He'd made the threat with one of his old man's rifles pointed at his daddy's head when his father had roused from one of his drunken stupors.

It was the first time his father had actually looked scared. And the first time Johnny had realized that he had it in him to kill a man.

Now he lay in bed sweating and staring at the wall.

He should have pushed Rachel for the truth about her name and her past.

But he hadn't had the heart. Not after witnessing the terrified look on her face when she'd seen that snake.

Kenny troubled him even more.

The sun wove through the blinds and he rubbed his eyes, then climbed from bed and showered, tugged on jeans and a denim shirt, then headed to the dining hall. Since Rachel had started work at the ranch, he'd decided to eat with the other hands and campers instead of in the main house.

Building relationships and trust took time, and letting the boys and workers see him as accessible, not some wealthy rodeo star who just dropped in to make an appearance, was a first step.

Besides, the clock was ticking. His volunteer time on the ranch was limited. Soon he had to return to his own spread and take care of business. Spring roundup and breeding was upon them. And he had cattle to move.

When he stepped inside the dining hall, the

scent of sizzling country-fried ham and red-eyed gravy wafted toward him. He damn near burst from the intoxicating smell.

Hiring Ms. Ellen was the best choice he'd made so far. It was a good thing he got his exercise working the ranch or he'd be blimping up from eating her homemade cinnamon rolls, gravies and pies.

He glimpsed Rachel heaping scrambled eggs into one of the serving bins underneath the warming lamps, and noticed dark circles beneath her eyes. She yawned, and he realized she hadn't slept any better than he had.

Because of the snake, or whatever she was running from?

Anger knotted his stomach. Dammit. He wanted to know the truth, badly.

Laughter erupted in one corner, and he spotted Ricardo, the boy who'd been rude to her the night before, huddled at a table, a smirk on his face as he watched Rachel.

Suspicions reared their ugly head. Johnny had been a troubled kid himself—and a troublemaker. He recognized the signs of one in the making. And this one seemed to have his eyes set on picking on Rachel. Reining in his temper, he strode toward the table of boys.

Had he put the snake in her bed as some kind of prank to scare her?

Whether he had or hadn't, he would set the boy straight.

He grabbed a cup of coffee, saw Kenny talking to some of the younger boys, then headed to the corner group. They were chowing down, talking about the rodeo.

He snapped his fingers. The rodeo—that was his bargaining chip.

"Hey, guys," Johnny said as he slid into a seat. "Ready to start practicing?"

Three of the teens, Juan, Samuel and Devon, nodded.

"I want to learn how to pen," Juan said.

Samuel poked Devon in the side. "And we want to barrel race."

Johnny laughed. "Spoken like cowboys."

Ricardo remained quiet, tearing off a piece of ham with his fingers and jamming it into his mouth.

"Listen, boys," Johnny said. "We had a little problem last night. Do you know anything about it?"

A devil-may-care attitude colored Ricardo's eyes, but the other boys looked away guiltily.

"What kind of trouble?" Ricardo asked, puffing up his chest.

"Ms. Simmons found a snake in her bed." Johnny sipped his coffee but stared dead-on at Ricardo over the brim of his mug. "Funny thing is, I checked the cabin and didn't see how it could have gotten in. Not unless someone put it there."

Ricardo shrugged and wolfed down his biscuit.

"You know, Ms. Simmons is a nice lady. And she's here to help, so if anyone hurts her or messes with her, they'll answer to me."

"What you gonna do?" Ricardo asked. "Beat up on us like our folks did?"

Johnny sucked in a sharp breath, wondering if this had been a test for him. "No," he said calmly. "That's not how we do things around here." He gave him a pointed look. "But we also don't condone harassing or frightening the employees, especially women."

"It was just a dumb prank," Ricardo muttered.

Johnny gripped his mug to keep from boxing the kid's ears. "Maybe to you, but not to her. And in my book, any boy who gets his kicks out of scaring girls or women is not a man."

The other boys looked contrite, and Ricardo's tough-guy look crumbled.

"I realize you boys have suffered some hard knocks in your life." He swept his gaze across the group. "So did I. I also made mistakes and some stupid choices, but we're offering you a second chance." He set his coffee mug on the table with a firm thunk. "What you do with it is up to you. But if you want to stay and participate in the rodeo, you'll follow my rules. And you will respect the staff."

"Yes, sir," the other three boys said at once.

Ricardo chugged his orange juice.

"Do you understand?" Johnny said pointedly.

"Yeah, sure," Ricardo said.

"Yes, sir," Johnny corrected.

Ricardo shifted. "Yes, sir."

Johnny nodded. "Do you want to participate in the rodeo?"

Ricardo's defiant expression faded. "Yes, sir."

"Then apologize to Ms. Simmons."

Ricardo picked up his tray. "Yes, sir."

Maybe the kid just needed a little extra attention. He'd do what he could.

But if Ricardo pulled another stunt, he'd send him back to the orphanage. It would be a hard lesson, but some kids were like him. They had to learn the hard way or it didn't stick.

Johnny's cell phone buzzed, and he checked the number. Brody.

He stepped away from the table for a moment, then clicked to answer. "What's up?"

"Trouble at the north end. Fencing is down, looks like it's been cut."

Johnny glanced at Ricardo as he emptied his trash and wondered if he was responsible for this trouble, too.

"I'll round up some boys to help repair it," Johnny said.

Ricardo was heading toward Rachel, but he caught up to him. "Ricardo, hold up."

The teen looked at him with an anxious expression.

Johnny cleared his throat. "Some fencing was cut in the north pasture. Do you know anything about that?"

Ricardo's eyes sharpened defensively. "No, sir."

Johnny narrowed his eyes. "Are you sure, son? This wasn't another one of your stunts?"

Ricardo gave a vigorous shake of his head. "I'm sure, I put the snake in Ms. Simmons's bed, but I swear I didn't tear up no fence." Ricardo stuffed his hands in his pockets, and Johnny couldn't help but notice they were scarred and shaking. "I'll help you fix it, though, if you want."

Johnny studied him for a moment, but realized he believed the kid. "Thanks. Now make that apology and we'll ride out to the pasture together."

Ricardo looked relieved, then headed over to Rachel. Johnny remembered seeing that truck parked on the hill in the distance the night before. He'd thought it seemed odd but dismissed it.

Maybe whoever had been in that vehicle had vandalized the property. But who?

Brody's concerns about their neighbor Copeland needled him.

What if Copeland had hired someone to cause trouble?

RACHEL WATCHED sixteen-year-old Ricardo approach with a sense of dread. She'd seen Johnny talking with him, and wondered what was going on.

"Ms. Simmons?" Ricardo shifted back and forth from side to side.

Johnny stood by the wall, quiet but watching, arms folded.

"Did you need something, Ricardo?" Rachel indicated the trays of bacon, ham and eggs. "Another serving?"

He shook his head. "No, ma'am. I…" He cut his eyes toward the floor. "I'm sorry. I put that snake in your cabin."

His statement took her by surprise. She'd contemplated packing up and leaving today for fear Rex had found her. But then Kenny had jumped out of bed talking about his first riding lesson today, and she hadn't had the heart. Still, most of her clothes remained packed.

"You did?" she finally asked.

He nodded, then lifted his gaze to hers, his eyes wary. "It was just a prank, but Mr. J. said it wasn't funny and I had to apologize."

"Maybe it was funny to you, but it's not fun to be on the other end of a joke." She paused, caught Johnny's worried look, realized she sounded harsh, then softened her voice. After all, Ricardo was just a kid. No telling what he'd been through. And if this was Kenny, she'd want someone to give him a break. But they couldn't allow him to get away with it either. "Has that ever happened to you?"

He nodded, then gripped his hands together in front of him and stared at his feet.

Rachel's heart softened at his body language. According to Ms. Ellen, Ricardo lived in an orphanage and had been shuffled in and out of foster care since he was three.

Probably where he'd received those nasty scars on his hands. Abusers manipulated their victims to the point that Ricardo probably blamed himself and suffered from low self-esteem. Maybe he'd thought pranking her would earn him attention from the other boys.

"It takes a big man to admit his mistakes, Ricardo." Rachel patted his shoulder. "Now, how about an extra muffin?"

A small smile touched his mouth, revealing a missing tooth in the front. "Yes, ma'am. Thank you."

She handed him a blueberry muffin, and he

wrapped it in a napkin, then tucked it in his pocket.

Was he storing it for later because he'd gone hungry before? Her chest tightened. She'd make sure he received generous portions from now on.

As soon as Ricardo disappeared outside, Johnny approached her.

"You talked to him?" Rachel asked.

Johnny nodded. "I don't think he'll mess with you again."

Rachel nodded, then glanced at Kenny, who was emptying his tray.

"Is something else bothering you, Rachel? You don't look like you slept well."

Rachel bit her lip. She would have slept better if Johnny had stayed last night. But then, she might not have wanted to sleep.

And the thought of letting a man touch her, get close to her, scared her more than the snake.

"If you're in trouble, Rachel," Johnny said in a deep voice, "let me help."

She sucked in a sharp breath. Why did his gruff voice make her want to open up?

But Kenny raced toward her with an excited gleam in his eyes, and she clammed up. How could she tell Johnny that she was wanted by the law?

He'd call the police, then she'd go to jail and lose Kenny for good.

Kenny tugged at her hand, saving her from answering. "Mom, I'm gonna practice tying knots with the day troopers." He turned hopeful eyes at Johnny. "Then we'll have the riding lesson?"

Johnny tipped the brim of Kenny's hat. "Yep, this afternoon. I have to mend some fences this morning."

Rachel noticed the hero worship in Kenny's eyes and wondered if she'd made a mistake by coming here. "Have fun, Kenny. But remember, do what the counselor says."

He nodded and beamed a smile, then jogged to catch up with Blair, the camp counselor leading the group.

"Rachel?" Johnny asked.

Torn over wanting to accept his offer to help and the need to protect herself, she averted her gaze.

"Ms. Ellen and I need to clean up. But I'd like to watch the lesson with you and Kenny later."

"Sure." He looked slightly disappointed, but she hurried away before she did something stupid like confess the truth.

Kim and Lucy passed her, and Lucy waved, but Kim's curious look made Rachel wonder if Johnny had shared his suspicions with her. Desperate to shake her nerves, she joined Ms. Ellen and they worked in tandem making soup and sandwiches for lunch.

"Feeding this crew is a job," Ms. Ellen said in a blustery tone. "But I love cooking and these kids." A sad expression drew Ms. Ellen's usual smile into a melancholy moment. "You know, I lost a boy years ago. Just took off with the wrong crowd and he never came back."

Rachel's heart ached, and she put her arm around the older woman. "I'm so sorry, Ms. Ellen. Do you know what happened to him?"

Ms. Ellen wiped at a tear on her cheek. "Ended up dying in a car accident. Worst part was that I never got to tell him how much I loved him." She sighed heavily. "And that I forgave him for running away." She clutched Rachel's hand. "Sometimes, child, you got to just snatch the moment. And when you love someone, you gots to tell them 'cause you never know how long they'll be around."

Rachel squeezed Ms. Ellen's hands. She sensed Ms. Ellen was trying to give her advice, and she wished she could trust her heart enough to confide in this woman about her past. And to allow her budding feelings toward Johnny to grow.

But Rex would find her, and then she'd be sorry if she'd opened up to anyone else.

They both fell silent as they finished preparing the meal. If only her life here could last.

By the time she'd finished making the soup, she'd splattered tomato juice all over her shirt. So she walked back to the cabin to change before the lunch session began. But the moment she stepped inside, an eerie premonition skated up her spine.

The faint scent of a man's cologne again...only this time it was different. Not the usual one Rex wore. Had he changed, or had someone else been inside the cabin?

The hairs at the nape of her neck bristled, and she swung around to check the corners of the room. Someone was watching her....

She could feel it. Sense their eyes on her back.

Her pulse clamored as she scanned the living area and kitchen, but she didn't see anyone. Only, something seemed different. Had she left that coffee cup on the counter this morning? And that knife...

No...she'd put her cup in the dishwasher. And the knife...she hadn't used it for anything. And Kenny knew better than to play with sharp knives.

Anxiety knotted her shoulders, and she grabbed the knife and clenched it in case of an attack. Then she tiptoed into the hall to check the bedrooms. A twig on the floor caught her eyes, then dirt.

A footprint.

Too big to be Kenny's or hers.

Someone else had been in her place.

Was he still here?

Inching forward, she peeked inside Kenny's

room, but it was empty. His pj's lay on the floor beside the bottom bunk where he'd slept. His stuffed animals and cowboy toys were on the top bunk, staged as he'd left them when he'd set them up that way.

She moved slowly into the room and checked the closet, then breathed a small sigh of relief when she found it empty.

Her hand trembled as she forced herself to return to the hall and look into the room where she'd slept. Her stomach clenched as she scanned the area.

Her clothes had been rustled through in her suitcase, some of her underwear tossed about.

Her breath caught.

And a pair of her red lace panties had been ripped and were shredded across the white lacy sheets on the bed.

THERE WERE FOOTPRINTS around the broken fencing.

Johnny knelt and examined them, anger railing through him. Brody had insisted on installing state-of-the-art maintenance-free fencing made of a high-density polyethylene, or HDPE. It was brand-new.

Which meant that this section had definitely been sabotaged.

Furious, he scanned the land beyond the pasture

and realized several cattle had escaped because of the opening.

Brody had hired a couple of ex-cons, mostly misdemeanor records, no felonies, but he'd wanted to give them a second chance.

Could one of the employees have done this? Maybe one who was working for Copeland?

"We can fix it?" Ricardo asked.

Johnny nodded. "Yes. Then we'll round up the cattle that strayed from the herd."

Ricardo nodded, then Johnny strode to his pickup to retrieve his tools.

He and Ricardo worked for the next hour repairing the fence, then Johnny drove Ricardo back, saddled his favorite stallion, Soldier, and a quarter horse for the boy, and they rode out to corral the herd.

By the time they finished and had returned to the main house, it was lunchtime and he was sweaty and tired. But he was determined to figure out who'd sabotaged the fence, so he hurried to his office to search through employee records.

Even if he didn't find anyone suspicious from the preliminary background checks, he might determine who'd been driving that vehicle the night before. That person might have seen something, somebody who didn't belong.

Three men on the list had records. The first one a DUI, the second a vandalism charge, and the third, charges of petty larceny and assault, although the assault charges had been dropped. He cross-checked each name with the job assignments and work schedule, then perused their personal information for the type of vehicles they drove.

The man with the petty larceny record and assault charges, Frank Dunham, drove an SUV. Could he possibly be working for Copeland?

Johnny ran a search on Dunham and minutes later muttered a curse. Frank Dunham had served time in the state pen with Carter.

Dammit. Carter had been furious when Johnny had visited him. He hated him and Brandon. Would he sabotage the ranch to get revenge?

REX STUDIED THE DOSSIER his friend had printed out on Johnny Long, a litany of curses spewing from his mouth.

Damn cocky bastard had won a slew of rodeo awards and was a hero in the circuit. He had money coming out of his ass and enough land for an army to live on. He raised prized stallions, bred horses for racing and stud fees, and raised prime beef cattle.

And from the damn news article about this BBL place, Johnny Long was not only one of the fundraisers, but he'd also donated a million dollars to back the ranch and kid camps himself.

All to make himself look like some kind of damn saint.

But Johnny Long was no saint.

Rex could look into his eyes and see the evil. He skimmed the man's background and read that he'd grown up dirt-poor with a drunken, abusive father and a mother who'd run off and left him. Johnny had also tangled with the law himself and had liked bar brawls a little too much when he was young. He'd escaped jail time by the skin of his tanned, leathery face.

Rex flipped through the photographs of all the groupies who'd flung themselves at him. Women who would drop their pants for him at the crook of his finger.

He'd charm their clothes off with his shiny belt buckles, his smooth talking and awards and cocky grin.

Was that what he was doing to Rachel? Charming his way into her bed? Had she already succumbed to the man and become another whore for him to brag about?

And his son?

What the hell was she doing taking his son into another man's place to live?

"You want me to take care of Johnny Long?"

Rex shook his head, then unfolded a wad of cash and paid his buddy for the information. He'd already sworn him to secrecy.

Any man who broke that code would end up dead and his buddy knew it.

The man stuffed the money in his pocket, then slid into the shadows of the bar and out the back door.

Rex crushed the damn dossier in his hands, polished off his whiskey, then waved the waitress over for another.

If Johnny Long thought he was going to steal his wife and son, he was a fool.

By God, he would kill the son of a bitch and make Rachel watch. Then she'd beg him to take her back just to save herself from what he planned to do to her.

Chapter Seven

The fact that Frank Dunham had served time in jail with Carter seemed too coincidental for comfort and raised ugly suspicions in Johnny's head.

He checked his watch. Lunchtime. He'd already posted a note to the ranch hands and staff requesting a meeting to discuss the rodeo plans, so Dunham should be there, as well.

After the meeting, he'd confront the ex-con about the fencing. If he was in cahoots with Carter to cause trouble, Dunham's second chance would be gone. And Johnny would be heading back to the state pen to have a chat with his once-best friend.

Remembering Rachel, he washed up and changed his sweaty shirt. Not that he wouldn't dirty another one this afternoon, working with the horses, but he hated to go to dinner smelling like an animal.

By the time he arrived at the cafeteria, it was packed with campers and hands. Starved, he grabbed a tray and loaded it with a bowl of soup, two roast-beef sandwiches and a glass of sweet iced tea. He spotted Kenny talking and laughing with the day campers, then joined Brody at a corner table.

"I fixed the fence," he told Brody. "There was definitely foul play."

"One of the kids?" Brody asked.

He shrugged. "I don't think so. I checked with the counselors and they were all accounted for. I'm going to question one of the ex-cons we hired."

Brody cleared his throat. "I'm worried about Copeland. What if he's hired someone to make us look bad before the rodeo?"

Johnny considered the possibility. "He's worth checking out."

Brody frowned and dug into his food. "By the way, we have more sponsors for the rodeo, and a local reporter named June Warner is going to publicize the event. She's bringing a crew to interview you and film some of the campers and activities." Brody grinned. "So put on the charm, Johnny."

Johnny winced and wolfed down his sandwich. The BBL needed publicity for the rodeo, but he hated to put himself in front of the camera. He'd been thrown in the slaughterhouse before and it hadn't been pretty.

"Maybe you'd better handle this June person,"

Johnny suggested. "Not everyone in the media likes Johnny Long."

"Forget about the ones who slammed you. You've got hundreds of fans who love you, so show them what you're made of, Johnny."

Johnny sipped his tea. "Yeah, I guess you're right." Maybe it was time to man-up in front of the press.

"Speaking of the media, I see June now." Brody waved at an attractive blonde in a black pantsuit in the doorway. A cameraman stood beside her, but in spite of Johnny's conversation with Brody, his defenses rose.

He'd been annihilated once, but that had been a personal attack. It had hurt his career, but no one else suffered. This time, if he was crucified, the publicity might affect the BBL.

Then, you'll have to make sure that doesn't happen.

Brody waved his hands to quiet the group. "This is June Warner and her cameraman, Robbie," Brody said as he introduced the reporter. "They'll be talking to everyone, employees and campers. Be sure to tell them what you like about the camp and forget your complaints."

His comment earned a round of chuckles as he'd obviously hoped.

Johnny spotted Rachel watching, and noticed that she kept fidgeting. And when Brody mentioned that June would be talking to everyone, she ducked into the crowd as if she wanted to hide from the reporter. Why would Rachel avoid the media?

Because she didn't want her picture to show up in the paper? His jaw hardened. That might alert whomever she was running from where she was hiding....

Brody finished, then handed Johnny the mic, jarring him from his thoughts. "I appreciate all the hard work everyone has put in to make our first camp a success." Johnny scanned the boys' faces. "And you guys and girls are doing a great job helping to make this ranch run smoothly."

"When's the rodeo gonna be?" a boy named Willie, in the front row, asked.

Johnny grinned at the handicapped ten-year-old. A car accident had severed his right hand, but the kid was tough and was learning how to manage. "Two weeks. That doesn't give us much time to prepare."

Lucy waved her hand to get his attention, her red head bobbing excitedly, and Johnny's heart melted. "Yes, Lucy?"

"Are you gonna do trick riding, Uncle J.?"

Johnny nodded. "Yes, and I have some other friends from the rodeo circuit who will make special appearances. But you guys will be the highlight of the show."

"When do we start practicing?" another boy asked.

"How do we sign up?"

Johnny raised a finger to quiet them. "Let me tell you about the events, then you can try out different ones over the next few days. After that, you can choose the events you want to participate in." He glanced at Rachel. "Because the rodeo is open to the public, we plan to include activities for visitors, although they have to qualify, register and pay fees for the competitive events. We're also going to offer games for the younger kids. We'll have stick-horse races, pony rides, face branding, horseshoes, musical hay bales, a cactus hat throw and, of course, lots of food."

Ms. Ellen cleared her throat. "I'll help organize the food vendors."

Johnny winked at her. "Thanks, I knew I could count on you." He turned back to the group. "Now, for the competitive rodeo events. I'll post the lineup, but events include team roping, steer wrestling, saddle bronco riding, calf roping, bare-back riding, bull riding, barrel racing and cow penning."

A buzz of excitement rippled through the room as the boys began to chatter about the events.

Johnny met Rachel's gaze across the room and noticed a hesitant look in her eyes. She was going to stick around long enough for Kenny to take part, wasn't she?

A movement near the back caught his eye. Then he spotted Frank Dunham heading toward the back door.

"I'll coordinate with your counselors regarding a practice schedule and they'll work with you on making your choices." Johnny thanked them, then strode toward the back to catch Dunham. When they'd made it outside, he called his name.

"Frank, I need to talk to you."

The man pivoted and paused on the steps. He was tall, with dirty blond hair, scars on his forearms and eyes that looked worn down and defeated.

Johnny motioned for him to step aside so they couldn't be heard by the campers who were chattering in excited voices about the events as they poured from the dining hall.

"Dunham, we had some trouble up in the north pasture. Some fencing was cut and part of our stock got out."

A wary expression colored Dunham's face. "And because I have a record, you think I did it?"

Johnny shrugged. "I know you served time with Carter Flagstone, and he's pretty pissed at me and Brandon."

"I do know Carter," Dunham said, tilting his

chin, his eyes teeming with anger. "But I didn't mess with your fence."

Johnny gritted his teeth. "Carter didn't offer to pay you to sabotage our plans here?"

Dunham squared his shoulders, fisting his hands so hard that his knuckles bulged. "You've got it all wrong," Dunham said. "Carter told me about this place, but he did it as a favor."

"What do you mean, 'a favor'?"

Anguish lined the man's face. "Since I was released, my wife won't let me see my children. Carter thought if I helped out with the kids and proved myself, maybe the judge and my ex would change their minds."

Guilt nagged at Johnny. He understood the uphill battle in overcoming past mistakes. The entire premise of the BBL was built on aiding in that fight.

"The last thing in the world I'd do is jeopardize the rodeo and what you're doing for these children." Dunham's mouth flattened. "But if you don't believe me, I'll leave right now."

Johnny stared at him for a long minute. He did believe him. "No, that's not necessary. But do me a favor. If you see anyone messing around, let me know."

RACHEL AVOIDED JUNE WARNER as she scooted through the crowded room to interview the boys.

If the woman posted a picture of her or Kenny on the news, Rex would know where they were.

Then they'd have to leave.

The scent of hay and fresh-cut grass wafted around her, the clean, fresh air a reprieve from the hot kitchen and the odor of that cologne she'd detected in her cabin before lunch.

She scanned the land near the riding pens as she approached, her nerves on edge as she remembered the panties shredded on her bed.

Had Rex found her, or was that another one of Ricardo's stunts?

No…she'd heard Ricardo talking about being with Johnny in the north pasture to repair some fencing all afternoon.

Maybe one of the other campers had played a joke?

She prayed that was the answer, but she had to remain alert.

Horses neighed and trotted across the field, enjoying their freedom, their manes dancing in the wind. A pang of longing mushroomed inside her. For the past two years she'd felt trapped, as if she was in a prison of her own.

Several riding pens had been built side by side with connecting chutes and corrals for use in the rodeo events. Johnny led a dark brown stallion from the barn, the animal's regal stance reminding her of Johnny himself. Big, strong, tough, invincible.

An amazing animal.

An amazing man.

Stop it, Rachel. Just because he's been nice to Kenny doesn't mean you should fall for him. You're a woman with a checkered past.

And an ex who wanted her dead.

Her stomach clenching, she scanned the horizon again, thought she saw something flicker in the sunlight on the hill to the east, then chastised herself for being paranoid. There were ranch hands and counselors everywhere. It was broad daylight.

She and Kenny were safe.

"There's an old cowboy's saying—'If you give lessons in meanness to people or animals,'" Johnny said to the group of boys, "'then don't be surprised if they learn them.'"

"What does that mean?" Kenny asked.

Willie, the ten-year-old with the missing hand, piped up. "If you're mean to animals, they'll be mean to you."

"That's right, Willie." Johnny gave him a thumbs-up.

"I'd never be mean to 'em," Kenny said, brushing at his cowlick. "I like animals."

Rachel's heart squeezed. Thankfully, her son had none of his father's violent tendencies in him.

"Good. Animals can sense if you like them or

if you're nervous," he said. "If they're intimidated or sense danger, they may bolt, kick or attack." Johnny showed them how to slowly approach the animal, then lowered his voice and stroked the horse's mane with his long, blunt fingers.

His voice was as gentle as his touch, igniting a sense of wonder inside Rachel. Rex had been a charmer, but he snapped on a dime.

Johnny was tough but maintained control. She'd seen photos of him bareback riding and wrestling a steer, and the man had plenty of brute strength. He just didn't use it against women and children.

The circle of boys watched intently as he demonstrated. "Each of our counselors will teach you how to saddle your own horse and groom them. Then we'll ride around the pen so you can become comfortable in the saddle. Tomorrow we'll take a short trail ride."

Kenny's face lit up with excitement as the group divided up with their instructors. Rachel was relieved to see that Johnny kept Kenny with him. Not that she didn't trust the other counselors, but Johnny was a pro.

As she watched him with her son, a dull ache pressed against her breastbone. Kenny needed a man's influence in his life.

A man like Johnny.

Would she ever be free to live her life without looking over her shoulder and being constantly on the run? Free to know that Kenny was safe? That Rex wouldn't concoct some phony charges against her and lock her away so he could steal Kenny?

Free to love again and build a home for her and her son?

JOHNNY'S PULSE POUNDED at the torn expression in Rachel's eyes. She loved her son dearly, but tension and fear lined her face.

He wanted to ride in and rescue her from her problems, but she obviously had put a padlock on the gate to her heart.

Those bruises rose in his mind to haunt him. Who had given them to her? An ex-boyfriend or lover? Her husband? Kenny's father?

The incident with the fencing struck him again, and his anxiety mounted. What if he tracked her here and cut the fencing to distract him? Because he wanted to get to Rachel?

He led the Appaloosa around the pen a couple more times, then brought him to a halt and patted his side. "Good boy, Dusty."

"That was the mostest fun I've ever had." Kenny leaned over and hugged the horse. "I love you, Dusty."

Johnny grinned, his heart melting at the sight of the boy's face. This was what he'd been missing in his life. Purpose. Meaning.

A family.

Sure, he had Kim and Lucy, but that was different. He itched to have a son or a daughter of his own.

Whoa...don't go there, man.

Not with this boy and his mother. Not when she has secrets in her eyes.

Not when you know she's told you lies.

Not when she might have a husband somewhere hunting her.

RACHEL HATED ALL THE LIES. Lying to Johnny. To Ms. Ellen.

And she hated that she'd forced her son to lie, too.

What would her parents think of them now?

Shame filled her. Kenny was so excited about the upcoming rodeo that he'd talked Rachel's ear off while she'd helped Ms. Ellen prepare dinner, thankfully oblivious for the moment of the turmoil eating at her.

The beef Stroganoff smelled delicious, the peach pies intoxicating, reminding her of the years before her parents died. And the family life she'd so wanted for her own.

Her mother had liked to bake, had especially liked apple-and-blueberry cobblers, although Rachel had favored peach. Ms. Ellen reminded her of home and grandmothers, of warmth and love.

All the things that had been missing in her life.

She helped Ms. Ellen serve the meal, watching with appreciation as the ranch hands, counselors and kids streamed in. All were excited, tired, starving from the fresh air and hard work. Kenny gravitated toward his new friend Willie, and Lucy tagged along behind Rachel's son as if he was a big brother.

Kenny finished eating, then ran over to her as she cleaned up.

"Mom, the counselor said I can bunk down with the other campers. They're gonna sleep outside in tents tonight. Is that okay?"

Rachel's heart clenched at the childish glee in his eyes. How could she deny him? Although, the image of that shredded underwear taunted her, and nerves crawled down her spine.

Kenny tugged on her sleeve. "Can I, Mom? Pleeeaase. They're gonna roast marshmallows and tell cowboy stories."

The counselors were hovering around the boys, and she relented. She couldn't put Kenny in a bubble his entire life or he'd be miserable.

"Of course, honey. But just mind the counselors and stay with the group."

Then Kenny hesitated, bouncing back and forth on his feet. "Oh, no, I can't go, Mom. I gots to feed Cleo and the pups."

Rachel ruffled his hair. "I'll take care of them tonight. You can check on them in the morning."

A smile burst on his face, tugging at her heart, and she gave him a big hug. Then he raced ahead and threw his arm around Willie as if they were best friends. Tears pricked the backs of her eyelids. Here Kenny had a normal life.

But when would it end?

She glanced around for Johnny, but he was at another table firming up the schedule with Brody. She'd met him the day before and learned the story behind the ranch—Brody had lost a brother years ago, and he was still missing. To fill the void, he'd dedicated the ranch to helping other boys in need.

Johnny looked so handsome and strong that, for a moment, she just paused to drink in the sight of him. To allow herself to fantasize about making a life here at the BBL. About seeing him as more than a friend.

Finally, her good sense kicked in, and she went to help Ms. Ellen. She had to ignore the desperate yearning she had to be with Johnny. Nothing would come of it but heartache for her and her son.

When she and Ms. Ellen finished, Rachel headed back to her cabin, enjoying the fresh air. But as she neared the cabin, her internal radar spiked, warning her she was in danger. That someone was watching her.

Following her.

Footsteps crunched on dry gravel. Twigs snapped. The husky whisper of her name rolled off a man's lips.

Rachel whirled around just as a shadow crossed in front of her.

Then a man gripped her by the neck and shoved her toward the barn.

Chapter Eight

Johnny glanced around for Rachel as he finished sketching out the event schedule with Brody, but she'd disappeared. Kenny had left for the campout and he knew she'd be alone.

Maybe if he approached her as a friend, she'd open up.

But just as he made it to the door, the reporter caught him. "Mr. Long, can I speak with you for a moment?"

Johnny gritted his teeth, then pasted on a friendly smile before he faced her. "Yes."

Her green eyes lit with a smile. "I'm June Warner."

"Yes, ma'am. Brody told me who you are."

Her brows furrowed slightly. "You don't want the press here?"

Johnny forced himself to take a deep breath. Too often, he'd spouted off the first thing on his mind and the press twisted it to make him look like a cad.

"We need publicity for the rodeo and to raise

awareness for the ranch," Johnny said. "But I want to make sure we're shown in a positive light."

"I'm not here to make trouble," she said tightly. "I came as a favor to Brody."

Dammit. He was making a mess of this.

"I apologize if I seemed rude, Miss Warner. I... you obviously know some of the things the media said about me before."

"And they weren't true?"

"Some of them were," he conceded. "I let fame go to my head for a while. I was cocky and a show-off in the arena." He paused, injecting sincerity into his tone. "But I'd never hurt a woman or a child. *Ever.* And this ranch—what we're doing—it's important. It means something personal to all of us who've invested in it."

She switched on a mini tape recorder and pushed it toward him. "Then give me a quote."

He gave a clipped nod. "Everyone deserves a second chance," Johnny said. "Kids and adults alike. That's what we're here for."

She smiled her thanks, then Johnny turned and hurried out the door. The night air smelled sweet with wildflowers, the moon breaking through the clouds, a few stars glittering against the inky sky.

His boots crunched gravel on the path, and he veered by the barn as he walked toward Rachel's cabin. A blue SUV was parked to the side.

Then he heard a scream from inside the barn.

Rachel...

He bolted into a dead run, pushed open the barn door to the sound of horses neighing and whinnying. A figure in the back corner moved, and something banged against a wood rail.

"Let me go," Rachel said in a shrill tone.

"Do what I say, baby, and we can work out a deal."

A scuffling sound followed, then a man's grunt of pain.

"You bitch!"

Johnny's blood ran cold as he strode to the back corner. The damn man had Rachel penned against the wall.

She shoved at his chest. "I said, let me go."

Fury surged through Johnny, and he yanked the man away from her. "What the hell do you think you're doing?"

The man whirled around, his scraggly hair sweaty, his eyes gleaming with anger. The bastard's name was Burgess. Johnny recognized him from the employee file photographs.

"She asked for it," Burgess snarled.

Rachel's startled eyes met his, and his gut clenched.

"What I heard was her asking you to leave her alone," Johnny said through gritted teeth. "Now you're going to jail." Johnny glanced at Rachel to make sure she was all right. She looked upset but thankfully unharmed.

A vein bulged in Burgess's thick neck, then he shot Rachel a challenging look. "Go ahead, call the law."

Rachel's eyes widened with panic. "No, Johnny, just let him go."

"Rachel, he attacked you," Johnny said. "You should file charges."

She folded her arms around her waist. "No, please, just make him go."

A smarmy smile slid across Burgess's face as if he'd won a victory, irritating Johnny even more. Johnny snatched the man by the shirt and hauled him toward the front, then shoved him through the door. "Is that your SUV?"

Burgess shot him a defiant gaze, then nodded.

"Get in it and get the hell off this ranch." Johnny tightened his hold on the man's collar, nearly choking him. "And if I ever see you anywhere near here or near Ms. Simmons again, you won't have to worry about the law. I'll take care of you myself."

"You have no idea who you're messing with." Burgess's face reddened as he glared at Johnny.

Johnny didn't take threats well. "And neither do you." Furious, he opened the door and tossed him inside.

Burgess cursed as he jammed the key into the

ignition, but he started the SUV and roared off leaving a cloud of dust in his wake.

Johnny waited until he'd disappeared, then turned back to Rachel. She was standing at the barn door, her face ashen, her expression reminding him of a scared animal ready to bolt.

He needed answers. He wanted to know the truth about her name and the reason for the bruises she'd had when she'd arrived. And he wanted to know why the hell she'd refused to call the law.

But she was trembling so badly that he couldn't force himself to confront her just yet. Or maybe he dreaded the truth.

So he strode toward her, then pulled her into his arms and held her tight.

RACHEL WANTED TO RUN. She *needed* to run.

To escape.

Because she desperately feared the man who'd cornered her in the barn knew her real identity.

And that he was working for Rex.

But she was shaking too badly to move, so when Johnny closed his arms around her, she collapsed against him and, for a brief moment, allowed herself to believe she was safe. That he would protect her and her son.

That the peaceful life she'd enjoyed the past few days could last forever.

"Shh, it's okay," Johnny murmured against her hair. "He's gone. He can't hurt you now."

A strangled sob lodged in Rachel's throat, but she swallowed hard, refusing to let it out. If she started crying, she might never stop.

Instead, she clung to Johnny, letting him stroke her back and hair and soaking in his strength.

As her nerves calmed, she became hyperaware of the man holding her. Of the musky, masculine odor radiating from him, a sultry smell that reminded her of what it could be like between a man and a woman when sex wasn't about control but about touching, comforting and giving pleasure.

But the memory of that creep grabbing her replayed through her mind, and she tensed, shutting down.

Then his threat. *You can't run forever. Be good to me and I won't tell anyone who you are.*

He had to be working for Rex.

On the heels of his voice, Rex's threat taunted her—*I'll kill you next time.*

"Talk to me, Rachel," Johnny murmured. "I know you're afraid of something, or someone. Let me help you."

No one could help her. The one private investigator who'd tried to had ended up nearly dead at Rex's hands.

Suddenly claustrophobic in Johnny's embrace,

she pushed against his chest. "I'm sorry...I need to go."

He eased away, but caught her arms, forcing her to look at him. "Trust me, Rachel. I'll protect you and Kenny if you'll just tell me what's going on."

The sincerity in his voice wrenched her heart. She ached to trust him, to fall back into his arms and let him make everything all right.

But how could Johnny fight her ex? Rex's connections ran as deep as his rage. For God's sake, his father had been a judge himself and had managed to pay off anyone who tried to tangle with his son. If Rex thought Johnny was involved with her, he'd kill him to get to her.

"That man just shook me up," she said, then glanced pointedly at his fingers where they held her. "Now, let me go, Johnny. I've been manhandled enough for one night."

Pain and regret flashed in his eyes and he instantly released her. "I'm sorry, Rachel. I...would never hurt you."

Her stomach knotted. He didn't deserve her harsh words, but she had to protect herself. She could not rely on him or confide the truth.

"A lot of men say that," she whispered in a raw voice.

Johnny's gaze met hers, understanding flickering in the depths. "Who was he, Rachel? Who hurt you? Your father? A boyfriend? Husband? Lover?"

She averted her gaze. She couldn't stand to see the pity in his eyes. She felt broken, damaged.

As if she'd never be able to love a man again, to give herself to him.

Which was fine. She had Kenny. Her son was her life.

"My personal life is not your concern," she said.

A muscle ticked in Johnny's jaw. "If it endangers the children and staff on this ranch, it is."

Guilt slammed into her. He was right. "I'm sorry. I didn't mean to sound like I don't appreciate you coming to my rescue. You won't have to do it again."

Her heart hammering in her chest, she brushed by him and hurried toward her cabin. Moonlight streaked the path, shimmering off pebbles, grass and twigs. The air smelled sweet with honeysuckle as a breeze stirred the trees. Stars glittered above, a perfect night for Kenny's campout.

She hated that it would be the only one he'd get to enjoy.

Behind her, Johnny's footsteps crunched the dirt, and she quickened her pace, then climbed the steps to the porch of the cabin. Johnny came up behind her as she unlocked the cabin door.

"What did you mean, I won't need to do that again?" Johnny asked.

Rachel walked inside, flipped on the lamp, then headed toward her bedroom. "It means I'm sorry there was trouble. Now please go, Johnny." She needed to pack.

But Johnny stood his ground. "I'm not going anywhere until you explain what's going on."

Rachel closed her eyes and said a silent prayer for strength, then spun around. "Look, I understand your concern about the boys here, and believe me, the last thing I would want is to endanger a child." Or you.

Because she was starting to really like Johnny Long.

He wasn't the cocky, arrogant bastard the papers had pegged him to be. He was caring and protective and a good role model for these troubled kids.

Especially her son, who certainly hadn't had a father figure in Rex.

Johnny's eyes bore into hers. "I believe that, but I also know you're in trouble. What are you running from, Rachel?"

"Nothing," she said with an edge to her voice. "But if you feel I'm a threat, Kenny and I will leave in the morning."

She reached in the closet for her suitcase, deciding to pack the few things she'd removed so they could get an early start. Breaking the news to Kenny, picking a new name and a new destination would be difficult, but she'd make him understand.

Johnny caught the bag in his hand. "I don't want you to leave."

Their fingers brushed, stirring long-dormant desires to flutter in her chest.

"Why, Johnny? You won't have trouble finding another cook."

The air vibrated with tension as his gaze locked with hers. She wanted to believe that he cared. But how could he when they barely knew each other?

"Just think about Kenny," he finally murmured. "He's so excited about learning to ride, you can't tear him away before the rodeo."

Pain and guilt squeezed her chest again as she searched for a reply.

Then he brushed his knuckle across her cheek. "Stay."

His husky tone washed over her, triggering crazy thoughts of want and love and the desire to fall into his arms again.

He inched closer to her, so close that she saw the raw need in his expression, the hunger building in his eyes.

Her body trembled with a heat of its own, and she ordered herself to pull away. To tell him to leave.

But when he cupped her face between his hands

and lowered his mouth to hers, she closed her eyes and silently pleaded for his kiss.

KENNY SETTLED NEXT TO Willie around the campfire, excited about the campout. But one of the campers was telling a ghost story about a little kid being lost in the woods, and a monster chasing him, and he couldn't help but peer around through the trees.

Yesterday he thought he'd seen a big man watching him at camp. And the day before, he'd heard footsteps behind him. Another time he'd spotted a man on a horse trailing behind when he was riding with the other boys.

Eyes seemed to glow out of the darkness, and he shivered, pulled his knees to his chest and wrapped his arms around them.

"And the monster grabbed the little boy and dragged him into the cave—" the boy continued.

Kenny's stomach knotted into a ball, and he huddled closer to Willie. He was safe here with the other boys. He wouldn't go off alone just in case.

But what about his mama?

Tears burned his eyes. He wanted to stay here and camp with the boys. But maybe he should go back to the cabin.

She was all alone tonight. What if his daddy found her and came back and hurt her?

Chapter Nine

The yearning inside Rachel mounted as Johnny's lips claimed hers. His touch was gentle yet
firm, and he traced his tongue along her lips as he
pulled her into his arms. Craving more, she parted
her lips, inviting him to explore deeper, savoring
the taste of his masculine strength and desire.

Her soft sound of pleasure triggered his own
gruff one, and he increased the pressure of his
mouth against hers and stroked her back, press-
ing her body into his. The hard planes of his chest
brushed her breasts, his thick sex bulged in his
jeans and hardened against her thigh.

She threaded her fingers in his dark hair and
was rewarded when he trailed his lips down her
throat, leaving hungry kisses and nibbles as he
tasted the sensitive skin of her neck. One hand
snaked down to rub her hip, slowly, languidly, as
if he had all the time in the world, as if giving her
pleasure drove his own desires.

She clung to him, aching for more, to have his

skin against her own, to have his hands love all the secret places that longed for a man's touch.

Then his mouth paved a fiery path down her throat to her breasts, and her body burst to life as if he'd lit a fire inside. Tingling with sensations, she threw her head back in offering and allowed him to unbutton the top buttons of her blouse. Again, he moved slowly, tasting her skin inch by inch, his coarse, passionate whisper spiking her own.

Then one hand closed over her breast, massaging, stroking through the sheer lace of her bra. Even as her nipple stiffened, throbbing for his mouth, reminders of Rex's rough handling broke through the haze of arousal. She fought to stifle them, but the moment Johnny backed her against the wall, panic shot through her.

She hated to be penned in. Held down. To be at the mercy of a man.

"Please…stop…"

Her raspy breathing turned to a painful gasp for air, and she pushed against his chest.

He leaned back, his eyes dark and feral, pupils dilated with hunger. But concern registered in his expression, followed by questions that she didn't want him to ask.

Questions that triggered her shame.

A heartbeat of silence stretched between them, but he didn't speak. Instead, he lifted his thumb and brushed her cheek with the pad, slowly, sensually, so heartachingly tender that tears blurred her eyes.

"I'm sorry you've been hurt," he said gruffly, then took a step away. "But I promise, I will never hurt you, Rachel."

The sincerity in his husky vow made her want to drag him back in her arms, made her wish she had the courage to confess everything.

Made her want to trust him with her story. With her body. With her heart.

But Rex had hurt her too badly to do any of those things.

"Please," Johnny whispered, "tell me what you need."

What she needed was for him to hold her again, to make love to her and erase the memory of Rex's vile hands.

But she had to keep him at bay and guard her secrets.

Squaring her shoulders, she wrapped a firm band around her heart. "I'm fine, Johnny. I'm just tired."

Disappointment flared in his eyes, but he didn't push. Instead, he gave a clipped nod and walked toward the door. But just as he reached it, he turned back and looked at her one more time.

"Promise me you'll be here in the morning," he said softly.

Rachel's heart fluttered. She wanted to stay forever.

"For Kenny's sake," he finished.

She wet her lips with her tongue and tasted Johnny on her lips. The potent mixture of his tenderness and masculinity was enough to bring her to her knees. But the reminder of Kenny brought reality slamming into her hard.

Her main priority was to protect her son.

"For Kenny's sake," she murmured with a small nod of concession.

But if she discovered Rex was on the ranch, she'd forget that promise. For Kenny's sake, she'd run again.

And somehow she'd make herself forget Johnny.

JOHNNY'S BODY WAS WOUND tight as he left Rachel.

Dammit, this woman had him tied in knots. He wanted her with a vengeance. Her strength and that sweet vulnerability aroused both his lust and protective instincts, a lethal combination that he'd never experienced before.

He fisted his hands and strode back to his truck, then headed back to the main house. But he wouldn't be able to sleep, not with images of that animal pawing at her in the barn earlier.

Or the memory of her mouth seeking *his,* her hands drawing him nearer, her taste on his lips and her touch on his skin.

He needed to take a ride to clear his head.

He parked at the main barn, saddled up Soldier, then climbed in the saddle and galloped across the ranch. Ever since he was a boy, he'd felt at home in the saddle. One with the animal.

It was no different now. He guided the horse across the terrain, bypassing the stables and arena, then checked to make sure the animals they'd brought in for the rodeo had been delivered.

Satisfied to find things in order, he rode out to the north pasture again. He scanned the area to make sure the man who'd attacked Rachel hadn't decided to hide out somewhere on the ranch, then rode along the creek to the river.

He also looked for other signs of trouble in case Copeland had hired someone to sabotage them.

The rodeo was only a few days away, and Rachel had promised to stay until it was over. But what would happen then?

Dammit. He spun the horse around and headed back to the stables. If she wasn't going to confide the truth about her problems, he'd find out on his own.

He breathed in the fresh night air as he crossed the pasture, rode past the creek where the youth were camping out and slowed the horse, pausing to watch for a few minutes but staying hidden in the shadows. When he was a kid, he'd loved the outdoors, skipping rocks in the river, digging fence posts, diving into a haystack, but most of all, riding. God, he loved being in the saddle, the powerful feel of the beast beneath him.

It was the only time he felt in control.

He'd spent plenty of nights sleeping outdoors to avoid his father when he was on a tear. Camps hadn't been in the budget. And his old man wouldn't have sent him if it had been.

Laughter echoed through the trees, then voices as the group huddled around the campfire. He spotted Kenny sitting beside Willie, and smiled. Kenny didn't care that the boy was handicapped. In fact, he acted as if he didn't realize Willie's limitations, simply accepted him for who he was. Despite what had happened with Rachel, she had done a good job raising her son.

And the past few days Kenny seemed happy and relaxed, a far cry from the little boy who'd clung to his mother and looked terrified when Johnny had told him he had to earn his keep.

Memories bombarded Johnny. His father's drinking had made him violent. Too often he'd borne the brunt of his temper.

Had Kenny's father hit him, too?

The thought sent rage through him, and he whirled the horse around and galloped back to the stables. It took him a few minutes to unsaddle the stallion and brush him down, then he strode into the main house, snatched up the phone and punched in the number for the private investigator he'd used when his own troubles had nearly destroyed him. He didn't want to use the same service the ranch used for simple background checks. This had become too personal.

The P.I. answered on the third ring.

"Leon," Johnny said without preamble. "I need a favor."

"What's going on, Johnny? Somewhere else making up lies about you and trying to extort you?"

"No," Johnny said quietly. "But it is about a woman."

"Haven't you learned, Johnny? Women are always trouble."

A grin tugged at his mouth, but he remembered the bruises on Rachel's neck and it quickly faded. "Yeah, and this one has it written all over her."

A long-suffering sigh escaped Leon. "Hell, you're not going to listen to me anyway, so just spill it. What's her name and what does she want from you?"

That was just it. Rachel didn't want anything from him. Not his money or his help.

Which made him want to help her that much more.

"Her name is Rachel Simmons, and she has a six-year-old son named Kenny." A frisson of guilt assaulted him for betraying her, but he had to know the truth before he became involved with her.

Dammit. Who was he kidding? Foolish or not, he already was involved

"But I think she gave me a fake name," Johnny said. "I'm going to fax over a photo of her and the papers she signed when I hired her along with the social security number she put on her application. I want you to find out everything you can about her as soon as possible."

"Sounds serious," Leon mumbled.

Johnny chewed the inside of his cheek. He hoped to hell it wasn't, but he had a bad feeling.

Growing up with a hellion father, breaking horses, working the rodeo circuit and bull riding had taught him one thing—to rely on his gut instincts.

NIGHTMARES OF REX AND the man who'd attacked her in the barn plagued Rachel all night. Each time she jerked awake, she stared into the darkness searching for her ex-husband. Listening. Waiting.

By 2:00 a.m., she'd retrieved her gun and put it under her pillow. By five, she'd given up the battle for sleep, climbed from bed, showered, fed Cleo and the puppies, then hurried to the dining hall to help Ms. Ellen. With the counselors' assistance, the campers were cooking their own breakfast over the fire, so the group was smaller than normal.

A newspaper lay spread on the table where Ms. Ellen had been reading it. She glanced at the front-page article and staggered with shock at the photograph of the judge who had granted her divorce. Hands shaking, she sank into the chair and skimmed the article.

Police are investigating a double homicide at the home of Judge Walton Hammers and his wife. According to reports, they were held at gunpoint, Mrs. Hammers was tied and bound, then shot at point blank in the head, while her husband was shot in the abdomen and knee and bled out. There are no suspects at the time, but police are investigating the judge's previous cases. If you have any information regarding these murders, please contact your local police.

Rachel's head swam. Dear God. Had Rex done this? Killed the judge and his wife because he'd granted her the divorce?

Ms. Ellen bounded in, and Rachel struggled to pull herself together and went to work.

But every time someone entered the room, she tensed and checked to see if it was Rex.

Or Johnny.

She'd ached to have him hold her the night before and chase away her nightmares. An ache she couldn't assuage.

After cleaning up from breakfast, she hurried toward the pens where Johnny was working with the kids. Kenny waved to her from the opposite side of the fence where the boys watched Johnny leading Willie around on a gelding.

"I'm next, Mommy!" Kenny shouted.

Rachel smiled and gave him a thumbs-up. Since they'd arrived, Kenny had blossomed from a shy, nervous little boy who hadn't had friends to an outgoing kid with rosy cheeks and friends.

But if Rex had killed that judge and was on their trail, they couldn't stay.

Johnny led the horse to a standstill, then helped Willie down. "You're a natural," Johnny said.

Willie grinned as he jogged back to Kenny. They high-fived, then Willie exited through the gate to stand by the other boys. Kenny hurried to take his turn, bouncing on his heels as Johnny helped him into the saddle.

Emotions crowded Rachel's throat as Johnny spoke quietly to the horse. His calm but confident manner with the animals transcended to the children. He was a born leader.

She glanced around in search of Rex, but she spotted the reporter and cameraman approaching, and her pulse clamored. The cameraman lifted his camera to tape Kenny who looked like a little cowboy in his boots, jeans and Stetson.

Panic beat a staccato rhythm in Rachel's chest, and she swallowed hard to keep from shouting at the man not to take her son's photo. The last thing she needed was for her and Kenny's pictures to be plastered in the papers offering a road map for Rex to follow.

If she caused a scene, she would only draw suspicion to herself.

Maybe if she asked Johnny, he'd convince them to not print her son's photo. But what reason could she give him?

She'd have to think of some kind of lie.

Anxiety needled her as Kenny finished his riding lesson, but she tried to hide it as Kenny jumped down. The horse lowered his head into Kenny's palm and Kenny giggled, then looked up at her with such joy that a tingly warmth spread through her.

Johnny motioned to the boys. "Come on, guys, we're going to meet Elvis."

"Who's Elvis?" Willie asked.

"Our prized bull." Johnny led the boys from the riding pens toward a barn adjoining the rodeo arena, complete with holding chutes and smaller riding pens. The reporter and cameraman mingled with the boys, and Rachel followed at a distance, determined to avoid the media attention.

Kenny raced ahead and climbed through the fence.

"Wait," Johnny called. "Let me check the bull's pen."

But before he could enter the barn, a bull charged out. Rachel's heart raced with fear as the huge animal roared toward her son, dust flying from his hoofs, his tail sticking straight out.

Some of the boys shouted at Kenny. "Look out!"

"Elvis is in there!"

Kenny jerked his head up and froze, terror on his face as he spotted the bull. The animal's head was lowered in attack mode.

"Kenny!" Rachel took off at a dead run.

The bull paused in the middle of the arena several feet from Kenny, bellowed, arched his back and shook his head from side to side, sizing him up as he would a threat.

"Run!" Willie yelled.

"Get out!" another boy cried.

"No, Kenny," Johnny said in a calm voice. He threw his hand up and motioned for the boys to quiet. "Stay back, guys. And stand very still, Kenny. If you run or scream, he'll think you're playing and he'll chase you."

Rachel trembled, inching toward the fence, desperate to reach her son. But she didn't want to make matters worse.

Moving slowly, Johnny climbed the fence, speaking in a low, soothing tone as he dropped to the ground. The bull dug his feet into the dirt, throwing it over his back as he lowered his head again, hunched his shoulders and angled his neck to the side toward Kenny.

Terror gripped Rachel. What if the bull attacked before Johnny could reach her son?

Chapter Ten

Johnny's pulse ticked violently, but the only way to rescue Kenny was to remain calm. He'd been charged by a bull before and nearly lost his leg and his life. He couldn't let the animal hurt Kenny.

"You're doing great, Kenny," Johnny murmured. "Remember what I told you about animals. They attack if they feel threatened, and we're not going to let Elvis think we're out to hurt him."

"He looks mad," Kenny whispered.

"It's his nature. He hasn't been broken like the horses we've been riding." Johnny moved one foot forward slowly, then another, treading lightly, careful not to make any sudden noise. "In the rodeo, riders are timed to see how long they stay on him, so bucking is his job."

Kenny trembled. "I'm scared."

"I know, bud, but I'm not going to let him hurt you." Johnny edged closer, holding up a calming hand toward Kenny. A couple more feet and he could touch the little boy.

The bull pawed at the ground, then bellowed in attack mode.

Johnny's lungs tightened as he tried to control his own fear. Behind him, the tension was palpable as Rachel and the boys anxiously watched. Out of the corner of his eye, he spotted the cameraman recording every second.

Dammit. He couldn't lose Kenny.

And if that bull hurt him, it would be plastered all over the news. Everyone would see him as a failure, and believe the ranch was too dangerous for their kids.

Then the BBL would be doomed.

Another inch, then another. Time seemed to stand still.

"Please save him," Rachel whispered.

"It's okay, Mom," Kenny said in a hushed voice. "Mr. J. knows bulls."

The boy's simple trust humbled Johnny.

"No need to attack," Johnny murmured to the bull as he watched him paw the ground again. The bull cocked his head sideways and stared straight up at Johnny as if in challenge.

Johnny lifted Kenny from the ground. "We're going to back up slowly," he murmured. "Just hang on and we'll be out of the pen in no time."

Holding Kenny to his side like a rag doll, he crept backward. Behind him, the hiss of collective breaths being held taunted him. When he reached the fence, Rachel met him, and he lifted the boy over the rails into her arms. Rachel hugged Kenny against her, then he hauled himself up just as the bull charged.

By the time he dropped to the ground, the bull had raced across the pen and was bellowing and kicking dirt.

The boys broke into cheers. "Yay!"

"You saved him!"

"Way to go, Mr. J.!"

Johnny shrugged off their accolades, angling his head away from the cameraman who was snapping pictures of the rescue and the angry bull.

Tears sparkled in Rachel's eyes as she clutched Kenny to her. "Thank you," she whispered. "Thank you so much."

Johnny nodded, but now the danger was over and his adrenaline was waning, anger set in. The bull should have been secure in the pen. Safety was of utmost importance when working with animals, especially when children were involved.

How in the hell had he gotten out of his stall and into the arena?

A COLD SWEAT BROKE OUT over Rachel. She was trembling as she clutched Kenny, desperately trying to erase the horrible images that had seared her mind at the sight of the bull attacking.

"Oh, Kenny, I was so scared. Are you okay, honey?"

Kenny nodded against her, then pulled back, the fear evaporating from his eyes. "I was at first, Mom, but I trusted Mr. J."

She wanted to trust him, too. And he had saved her son's life.

Johnny met her gaze, the relief in his eyes mixed with other emotions she couldn't define. Worry? Anger?

Then he jerked his head toward the counselors. "Take the boys over to brush down the horses. I'll meet you in a few minutes."

Kenny wiggled free from her, obviously undaunted and ready to trail the group.

"Are you sure you don't want to stay with me?" Rachel asked. "That was quite a scare."

"Cowboys are tough, Mom." Kenny puffed out his cheeks. "I have to help Willie and the others."

Johnny placed a gentle hand on her shoulder. "You can't watch him every minute, Rachel."

Anger heated her blood. "My job is to keep him safe."

"He is safe," Johnny said. "But he also needs to be a kid."

Rachel glared at him. "I hardly think you're qualified to tell me how to parent, especially in light of what just happened."

Hurt flashed briefly in his eyes, and once again,

Rachel realized she'd gone too far. Johnny had done nothing but be good to her and her son. So why did she keep striking back?

Because she was afraid of trusting him, of falling for him and getting hurt....

"You're right," he said. "I'm sorry. But I do want what's best for the boys."

Rachel noticed the reporter watching them with interest and put some distance between her and Johnny.

She hadn't meant to make a scene. "I'm sorry, Johnny. I...didn't mean to be harsh. I...I was just upset."

"Don't worry about it." He lowered his voice. "I need to examine that pen. We can't afford another slip like that."

He didn't need to finish the sentence. His silent message echoed in her head—a slip like that could get someone killed.

Remembering the terror she'd felt a few moments before, she watched him go.

"Ms. Simmons?" June made a beeline for her. "That is your name, right?"

Rachel tensed. She wanted to escape, but avoiding the woman would only raise suspicion. "Yes."

"That was your son, Kenny, right? The little boy who almost got gored by the bull?"

Her choice of words made Rachel's heart pound

anew. "Yes, he's my son. But I'd appreciate it if you'd leave his picture out of your story."

June narrowed her eyes. "Why? I'm sure Kenny would like seeing his face on TV."

Rachel struggled for an answer. "He doesn't need a reminder of the scary incident on screen. Maybe you should just focus on Johnny and the fact that he was a hero."

"We do intend to show that he was, but your son—"

"Would be embarrassed in front of his friends." June frowned, but Rachel continued. "Besides, the investors at the BBL need publicity to build the camp's reputation." The wind tossed a strand of hair loose from her ponytail and she tucked it back. "If you show a child in danger, it might give the ranch a bad reputation."

June raised an eyebrow. "But if safety standards aren't up to par, shouldn't parents and professionals working with these groups be informed?"

Gravel crunched behind them and Johnny suddenly appeared. "I can assure you that this was an isolated event," Johnny said. "And I will personally see to it that safety precautions are rechecked." He gave Rachel a curious look, and she wondered if he'd overheard the first part of her conversation with June. "In fact, I'm going to have a powwow with the staff and campers and address safety precautions before dinner."

"What about your neighbor's concerns?"

Johnny narrowed his eyes. "What are you talking about?"

"Come on, Mr. Long," June said. "Rich Copeland has been very vocal in his feelings about the set-up here. He spoke to me personally just yesterday." She paused to take a breath. "Don't you think he has a right to be worried about the possibility of troubled boys or one of your employees endangering him or his property?"

"He's not in danger," Johnny said curtly. "We screen our staff, and our counselors are responsible for supervising the campers at all times."

"Then how did that bull get out?"

"I don't know," Johnny said in a clipped tone. "But I intend to find out."

June hesitated, then looked at Robbie. "Okay, that's a wrap."

Robbie began packing up his equipment, and June and Robbie headed toward their SUV.

"Thank you for defending the ranch," Johnny said after the press had left. "But why don't you want Kenny's picture in the paper, Rachel?"

Rachel swallowed hard. "Like I told June, he might be embarrassed."

Disbelief tinged his eyes. "Right." His clipped tone sounded angry.

"How *did* the bull get loose?" Rachel asked.

Johnny leaned close so as not to be overheard. "One of the boards in the pen was sawed through." He hesitated. "That neighbor June mentioned, the one who opposed our ranch, my guess is he hired someone to sabotage us in front of the press."

"Why didn't you tell her that?"

"If I incriminated Copeland without evidence, the jerk would probably sue me and Brody and shut down our operation, which would play right into his hands."

Rachel clenched her hands together. That sounded feasible.

But she still couldn't help but wonder about her ex. Rex had enjoyed tormenting her.

Would Rex sabotage the ranch to the point of endangering his own son just to scare her?

JOHNNY STRODE AWAY, irritated that Rachel wouldn't confide in him and worried about the upcoming rodeo.

If Copeland had hired someone to mess with them, he'd gone too far.

He sent a text to the counselors and ranch foremen to have everyone convene for a meeting before dinner.

Then he climbed in his truck, phoned Brody and filled him in.

"Dammit," Brody muttered. "I don't like this. Maybe we should postpone the rodeo?"

"No, then Copeland wins and the boys lose out," Johnny said.

"You're right." Brody grunted. "Maybe I'll have another talk with him and be able to convince him to leave us alone."

"I hope it works this time," Johnny said. "I'll have a sit-down with the boys, counselors and staff. Hopefully someone saw something and will come forward."

Brody cleared his throat. "Thanks, keep me posted."

He disconnected the call, then spent the rest of the afternoon working on the lineup for the rodeo, dropping by the small groups to oversee the practice rounds, and checking security measures. He carefully examined each pen and stall himself to make sure nothing else had been tampered with.

A team of ranch hands roped off areas for the events for the younger children while Kim helped two college counselors organize items for the stick pony rides, cornfield maze, the horseshoe toss, face painting and the other special events.

Another group worked to designate areas for the food vendors, which included a barbecue pit, Brunswick stew booth, cornbread counter, corn on the cob stand, cowboy caviar corner, Tex-Mex bar, along with several others. Other booths would sell souvenirs including cowboy hats, belt buckles, Western clothing, stuffed ponies and posters. Volunteers would hand out the programs, which also included information on the BBL.

Finally, it was meeting time. Johnny whistled to snag the group's attention.

As he explained about the problems, unease rippled through the room.

"Listen, guys, believe it or not, I was once your age," Johnny started, trying to address them with respect and understanding but also adopting a no-nonsense approach. "Everyone enjoys a good prank. I was known to pull a few myself." He hesitated. "But I also did some dumb stuff, which could have gotten someone hurt or worse, killed. If that had happened, I don't think I could have lived with myself."

He watched the faces, searching for guilty looks, whispers of a conspiratorial nature, any sign of the culprit in the crowd. But picking out one guilty face in a sea of kids who'd already seen more trouble and heartache in a lifetime that anyone deserved was hard. A lot of them were angry. Had chips on their shoulders. Had learned to lie and fake innocence to cover their butts. Some of them had had no guidance. Some wanted to save themselves from the brunt of a fist. And some were just plain rebellious.

Still, he had to make his point.

He cleared his throat, his tone firm. "But cutting fencing and breaking pens where dangerous animals can escape is serious business. I hope, and pray, that none of you had anything to do with this, but if you did, or if you know who was responsible, please come to me and we'll talk. We're here to have fun, but we also want to teach you how to become responsible men." He paused for effect. "If you work on a ranch or with powerful animals like horses and cattle, or intend to pursue the rodeo circuit, one of the first rules you learn is that safety is a priority. Never underestimate the power of an animal, in the pen, on a riding trail or in a rodeo arena."

Boys shifted. A few anxious whispers erupted.

"Now let's review safety precautions and rules for the rodeo events."

He displayed charts to illustrate his points and spent the next half hour discussing them and answering questions. By the time he finished, he hoped he'd instilled some healthy fear and respect into the crew.

"Remember, respect the animal and he'll respect you." Johnny smiled. "Then you'll respect yourself."

When he finally finished his talk, he decided to take another ride across the ranch to check things out. Then he'd circle back and walk Rachel and Kenny home.

Forty-five minutes later, night had set in, with heavy dark storm clouds brewing as he headed back to the dining hall. The inky gray seemed to stretch forever, giving the pastures and land an ominous, deserted feel.

Ms. Ellen honked from her Thunderbird as they passed each other, and he waved in return. Then he noticed a hazy fog in the distance near the dining hall.

Alarm rippled up his spine, and he pressed the gas pedal. Was that smoke?

Ms. Ellen had just left the dining hall. Wouldn't she have known if something was wrong?

His heart jumped to his throat, and he roared past the arena, frantically praying he was wrong. But the closer he got to the dining hall, the more his fears intensified. A thick plume of smoke curled against the darkness.

The scent of burning wood seeped through his open window, and sweat trickled on his skin as he roared to a stop. Flames danced along the back wall, racing upward toward the black sky...

Dammit. The dining hall *was* on fire.

Were Rachel and Kenny still inside?

Chapter Eleven

"Mom, there's smoke!" Kenny cried.

A shudder tore through Rachel as she jiggled the door to the walk-in pantry. "I know, baby, I'm trying to get us out, but the door's jammed."

Kenny coughed, and she tugged at the doorknob again, jerking with all her might, but it wouldn't budge. Meanwhile, smoke seeped below the crack in the doorway and was flowing into the storage room. The scent of burning wood and plastic filled the air, the crackle of splintering boards. The fire was growing stronger, traveling toward the pantry.

If she didn't get them out soon, they might die.

She felt for her cell phone but realized she'd left it on the kitchen counter when she'd stepped inside to unload the box of canned goods. Frantically, she glanced around, searching for a tool to help dislodge the door, or another escape route. A back door? Window? Another connecting room?

None of them.

Fear clawed at her, and she glanced up and spotted a vent. Could she crawl through it?

No, the vent was too small and narrow for her to fit.

Kenny doubled over with a cough, and her own eyes burned from the smoke. Then a crashing sound came from the kitchen. The ceiling? Burning boards?

Dear God, how was she going to save them?

Tears threatened, but she spotted several stacks of dish towels. If they could stay alive until someone spotted the fire, maybe they would be rescued.

She gestured toward the stack of dishcloths. "Kenny, grab those rags and stuff them at the bottom of the door to keep the smoke out!"

Kenny raced to do as she said, and she slammed her weight against the door, pushing it. "Help! Someone help us!" Again, she stepped back, then rammed her shoulder and body against the doorway, this time with such force that pain knifed through her shoulder blade and ripped down her arm. The wood was growing warm, too, heat radiating from the paneled door.

"Mom?" Kenny kept shoving towels in front of the opening, but he was coughing more violently now, and his cheeks were red from the heat. Outside the door, the blaze hissed louder and more wood splintered.

"Stay low," Rachel ordered, remembering that smoke rose and that the freshest air would be lower.

Frantic, she grabbed a broom and banged the door repeatedly, but to no avail. She spotted a handheld can opener on the counter and grabbed it. Maybe she could use it as a lever to pry open the door.

Kenny started kicking at the door and she beat it with her fists. "Help! Someone help!" Kenny shouted.

Sweat trickled down Rachel's chest and temple as she jammed the edge of the can opener into the door edge and pushed, but the door still wouldn't budge. Smoke stung her eyes, and tears caught in her throat. But she couldn't give up.

She kicked the door again, then grabbed the biggest can she could find and pounded the wood surrounding the doorknob, hoping if she kept it up, the impact might shatter the wood and make a hole big enough to slip her hand through.

Kenny lowered his head, coughing into his hands.

"Please, someone, get us out!" Rachel screamed. "We're trapped inside!"

Something crashed on the other side of the door, and terror seized Rachel. Even if they did get the door open, if the room was completely on fire, how would they escape?

JOHNNY CURSED AS HE shoved open the door and saw the flames dancing along the back wall near the kitchen. He scanned the large dining room to see if anyone was inside, but thankfully, it was empty.

Although sounds erupted from the back. Wood splintering. A crash.

He grabbed a fire extinguisher from one of the built-in emergency units, then punched Brody's number. "Brody, there's a fire at the dining hall."

Brody released a string of expletives. "How bad is it?"

"Just the kitchen now. I'll try to control it until the fire department arrives."

"Thanks. I'll call some hands to help and be right there."

Another banging sound echoed over the roar of the fire, and Johnny's chest tightened with fear.

Was that a voice?

Clutching the fire extinguisher with a white-knuckled grip, he hurried to the kitchen entrance. Flames chewed at the wooden beamed ceiling and floor and shot toward the pantry, and a smoky haze flooded the room making it damn near impossible to see.

But the pounding noise grew louder, and sheer panic knifed through him. Someone was trapped in the back in the pantry.

"Help, someone, help!"

"We can't get out!"

Dammit, it was Rachel and Kenny.

"I'm here," Johnny yelled. "Hang on and I'll get you out."

Flames blocked his way, but he had to get to the back. His heart pounded as he sprayed the fire with the extinguisher, clearing a path.

"Hurry!" Rachel cried.

More banging as they tried to open the door. Heat seared Johnny as he grew closer to them. Damn. How had they gotten stuck inside?

Sweat soaked his skin and hair, and his hands were shaking as he continued working to dowse the flames. Heat blazed, stinging his arms, but he finally plowed through and made it to the pantry. Johnny pulled at the door, but it wouldn't open.

"The door's jammed!" Rachel cried.

She and Kenny had wedged towels along the bottom to stifle the smoke. But judging from the coughing he heard inside, some was obviously seeping through.

"Hurry!" Rachel yelled.

Johnny jogged toward the emergency closet on the opposite side of the kitchen, unlocked the door and grabbed the ax he'd stowed there for emergencies. Wood splintered and he dodged a falling board, beating at flames licking the leg of his jeans as he ran back to the pantry door.

"Johnny?" Rachel's voice sounded raspy now as if she was growing weak.

"I'm here," he yelled. "Get Kenny and stand back as far as you can. I'm going to break open the door!"

Her footsteps shuffled from the inside. "We're against the back wall."

"I have an ax," Johnny shouted. "Cover your heads in case wood splinters fly!"

He waited a second, giving her time, but the flames had started climbing along the opposite wall now. "Ready?"

"Yes, just get us out!" Rachel shouted.

Sweat dribbled down his forehead to his eyes, and he swiped it with his sleeve, then swung the ax into the door near the doorknob. Wood splintered and cracked, and he swung it again, then again, knocking off the doorknob and surrounding wood.

Heat scalded his back as he ripped open the door. Rachel and Kenny were huddled in the far corner with Rachel protecting Kenny with her arms and body.

Emotions crowded Johnny's chest as he ran to them.

RACHEL'S EYES BURNED from the smoke, but relief poured through her as she looked up at Johnny.

Kenny coughed against her, but Johnny scooped him into his arms and grabbed her hand. "Come on."

Rachel felt dizzy, but she clung to his hand, covering her mouth with her arm to keep from inhaling more smoke as they raced through the kitchen. A section in the far corner was still aflame, but it looked as if Johnny had extinguished the fire near the pantry.

Johnny led them outside, and she dragged in the fresh air, her lungs aching. He carried Kenny to a giant oak far from the smoke and eased him to the ground. "Are you okay, buddy?"

Kenny was sweating and soot streaked his little face, but he nodded, his eyes huge as he glanced back at the dining hall. A truck roared up, then another, followed by an SUV, and Brody and four ranch hands jumped out.

Brody looked angry and worried as he jogged toward them. "Is anyone hurt?"

Rachel shook her head and pulled Kenny up next to her. "No, we're okay."

"I put out most of the fire, but there's still flames along one wall." Johnny motioned the ranch hands to follow him. "Come on."

Brody moved in front of him. "Stay here with Rachel and the boy and wait for the ambulance," Brody said. "I'll go."

Rachel clutched Johnny's arm. "We don't need an ambulance," Rachel said. "We're all right."

A muscle ticked in Johnny's jaw. "You're both going to be examined," he said firmly.

Rachel bit her lip to stifle an argument. She didn't want attention drawn to her and Kenny, or that reporter to get wind of this and expose them.

But Kenny *had* inhaled some smoke and looked pale. What kind of mother would she be if she didn't allow a doctor to examine him?

"I'll be right back." Johnny hurried to his truck, then returned a moment later with a water bottle and offered it to her.

"Thanks." She unscrewed the cap and gave it to Kenny. His hands were shaking, his complexion ashen as he turned up the bottle and drank.

When he'd taken a few sips, he handed it to Rachel and she drank slowly, grateful to soothe her parched throat.

Johnny stooped and tipped Kenny's face up with his hand. "Feeling better, partner?"

Kenny nodded, then swiped at the water dribbling down his chin with his hand. "It was hot in there."

"I know, buddy. The medics will be here in five minutes. Just rest till then."

The boy leaned back against the tree, and Johnny gestured to Rachel to step to the side.

"What happened? How did you and Kenny get trapped in the pantry?"

Rachel pushed a strand of hair from her eyes. "Ms. Ellen's back was hurting, so I told her to go home, that Kenny and I would stock the shelves before we left for the night."

Johnny nodded. "I passed her on the way to the dining hall. So she hadn't been gone long when the fire broke out?"

"No." Rachel's head felt foggy as she thought back over the details. "After she left, Kenny and I went into the pantry."

"Did you close the door?"

Rachel fidgeted. "Not all the way. But when Ms. Ellen left, it slammed shut. I figured the wind caught it as she went out the other door."

Johnny chewed over that possibility. "Then what happened?"

Rachel wrung her hands together. "Kenny and I were shelving canned goods, then I smelled smoke and tried to open the door, but it wouldn't budge."

"Did you hear anyone else inside the kitchen? Footsteps maybe?"

She strained to remember. But Kenny had been chattering away about the rodeo while they worked and she had let down her guard. "No. What are you getting at, Johnny? You think someone intentionally set the fire?"

The sound of a siren wailing rent the air, and

the ambulance raced down the drive, the fire engine on its heels.

"I don't know, but we've had two other questionable incidents lately, and this makes the third."

Earlier, Johnny mentioned his neighbor might be sabotaging the ranch. Had he set the fire?

Rachel's chest squeezed with panic. Or had Rex?

She'd known he would kill her if he found her. But would he really kill his own son?

JOHNNY WAVED THE MEDICS over to examine Rachel and Kenny, then led the firemen inside the building.

Brody looked up and greeted the firemen. "We extinguished the last strains of the fire, but we don't know what caused it."

"Captain Jim Madison," one of the firemen said. "If you don't mind, take your men outside, and let us look around for the point of origin."

Brody gestured to the ranch hands to go outside, but Johnny waited beside Brody as the men examined the scene. He wanted answers.

The scent of smoke and charred wood permeated the room, the memory of Rachel's screams for help haunting him.

"How are Rachel and Kenny?" Brody asked.

"The medics are checking them out now."

One of the firemen knelt to study the oven and floor surrounding it.

"That door was jammed," Johnny said to the captain. "I think the lock was broken."

Madison walked over to examine the door, then turned to Johnny. "You're right. Looks like the lock was jimmied."

Anxiety knotted his shoulders. Had someone intentionally trapped Rachel and Kenny inside the pantry?

The other fireman brushed aside debris and sniffed along the edge of the wall. "Captain, it smells like gasoline over here."

Brody's boots pounded as he followed the captain to the site. Madison knelt and studied the wall and floor, and Brody's expression grew strained.

"You're right," Madison said. "There was an accelerant."

Roy, one of the hands, poked his head into the door. "You want us to start cleaning up?"

"Not yet." Brody reached inside his pocket for his phone. "This fire was no accident. I'm calling the sheriff."

Johnny's gaze met Brody's, Copeland's name lingering in the silence between them.

Had he hired someone to mess with the fencing and the bull's pen and set this fire to force them to shut down?

Or was it the man after Rachel and Kenny?

Chapter Twelve

Brody released an exasperated sigh as he ended the call. "The sheriff's on his way."

"I need to speak to him when he arrives," Captain Madison said. "Meanwhile I'm going to take some samples to send to the lab."

Brody nodded, and he and Johnny stepped outside.

"Do you think Copeland is responsible?" Johnny asked.

Brody shrugged. "I don't know. I called him, but his housekeeper said he's been out of town for the last few days."

"Maybe he hired someone to do his dirty work and took a trip to give himself an alibi."

"That's possible. Although, if someone intentionally jammed that lock, we're talking attempted murder." Brody removed his hat and scrubbed his hand through his hair. "Anyway, I'll fill the sheriff in and let him handle the investigation."

Johnny shifted, his thoughts jumbled. He'd held

too much back from Brody. This incident was too serious to ignore. "There's another possibility."

Brody angled his head toward Johnny. "What?"

"One of our hands named Burgess assaulted Rachel in the stables."

Anger blazed in Brody's eyes. "What? Why didn't you tell me?"

"Rachel asked me not to," Johnny said. "She… said she just wanted to forget it. So I fired him, then let him go with a warning."

Brody folded his arms, his jaw hardening. "What's going on, Johnny? One of our employees attacks a woman and you don't call the cops or report it to me?"

"It was a bad judgment call," he said. "Besides, you've been worried about publicity and I was trying to respect Rachel's privacy."

"So you think this guy was pissed, and he could have come back for revenge?"

Johnny nodded.

"We need to give his name to the sheriff."

"I know," Johnny said. "Do you think we should postpone the rodeo?"

"No." Brody's tone was emphatic. "We're not going to let anyone destroy our operation. I'll hire extra security for the next few days."

"That might not be a bad idea, at least until we figure out who's behind all this."

Brody nodded. "Under the circumstances,

Johnny, you'd better keep an eye on Rachel and her son. If Burgess was responsible for the fire, he might try something else."

Johnny heaved a weary breath, contemplating whether to divulge his suspicions about Rachel's past, but decided he'd wait until he heard from the P.I.

No sense alarming Brody until he had more information in hand.

A car engine rumbled down the hill, and the sheriff's squad car flew down the drive, then he parked and climbed out. Johnny headed toward the ambulance where the medics were examining Rachel and Kenny. He didn't like dealing with the law himself, not after that fiasco with Gwen.

But this time, Rachel had to talk to the sheriff.

A strained look tightened her face, and she wrapped a protective arm around Kenny.

Johnny's boots crunched pebbles and grass as he cut across the path. Rachel might be scared. But what if other boys or staff had been inside the dining hall?

If she knew who'd set that fire, she had to speak up.

RACHEL FELT THE WALLS closing in around her. Someone had almost killed her and Kenny tonight. And now the sheriff had shown up and was making a beeline for her.

She had to cooperate and talk to him or raise suspicion. Then she had to leave the BBL.

Pain wrenched her heart. Kenny would be heartbroken....

God, she didn't want to face the police. Not with the guilt and lies choking her.

But Brody and the sheriff were near, and she couldn't run. The men reached her at the same time, and she shoved hair from her face and inhaled a calming breath.

Johnny glanced at the medics. "How're they doing?"

"Okay," one of the medics said. "The boy inhaled some smoke, but he seems fine now. His lungs sound good, and there are no cuts or burns."

"Good," Brody said. "But Rachel, it looks like the fire was intentionally set. Sheriff McRae needs to ask you some questions."

Rachel nodded, her worst fears confirmed. Someone had intentionally set the fire...with her and Kenny trapped inside. Was it Rex?

Johnny squeezed her arm. "I told Brody about Burgess."

Pure panic seized Rachel. He'd promised—

The sheriff stepped in front of her, cutting off their conversation.

"I need you to tell me what happened," the sheriff said.

Rachel clutched the blanket the medics had

given her around her shoulders. "I already told Johnny. Kenny and I were in the pantry stocking shelves when I smelled smoke."

"We couldn't open the door," Kenny piped in. "We shoved and pushed and Mommy tried to use a can opener to pry it open, but it wouldn't move."

"Did you close it yourself?" Sheriff McRae asked.

Rachel shook her head no. "We left it cracked, but when Ms. Ellen, the main cook, left, it swung shut. I figured it was the wind and didn't think anything about it. Not until we smelled smoke."

Sheriff McRae nodded, and Rachel barely resisted the urge to squirm beneath the scrutiny of all three men.

"You didn't hear anyone else inside?"

She shook her head, and he glanced at Kenny. "How about you, sport?"

Kenny clutched the water bottle Johnny had given him. "No, not till Mr. J. came and saved us."

Sheriff McRae turned a questioning look toward Johnny. "How did you know they were inside?"

"I didn't, not at first," Johnny said. "I was driving by when I saw smoke, so I stopped and ran inside. Then I heard Rachel and Kenny banging on the door and shouting for help."

Sheriff McRae folded his arms. "Ms. Simmons, can you think of anyone who'd want to hurt you?"

Rachel's pulse clamored. Just her ex-husband, the man who had promised to love, honor and cherish her. But if she revealed Rex's name, her freedom would be over.

So she clutched the blanket tighter. "No. Are you sure it wasn't faulty wiring?"

"I'm sure. We discovered an accelerant," Sheriff McRae said.

Brody cleared his throat. "What about the man who attacked you in the stables?"

Rachel shivered and gave a quick glance toward Kenny. She hadn't told Kenny and hated that Johnny had broken her confidence.

Johnny seemed to understand her concern for her son, and leaned over to Kenny.

"Hang tight, bud. We'll be right back."

He placed his hand on her back for support, and Rachel, Johnny, Brody and the sheriff walked a few feet away from Kenny.

"What attack?" Sheriff McRae asked.

Johnny quickly filled him in.

"Why didn't you report him, Rachel?" Brody asked.

Rachel struggled for a believable lie. "I didn't want to upset Kenny. Besides, I thought it was a one-time thing. The man smelled like he'd been drinking, so I just assumed he got carried away. I wasn't hurt, so no harm was done."

"What happened next?" Sheriff McRae asked.

"I fired him and gave him a warning," Johnny said.

The sheriff shifted, seemingly contemplating the situation and Johnny's response. "I'll need his background information, address, et cetera," the sheriff said.

Johnny gave Rachel's arm an encouraging squeeze. "I'll email it to you."

Brody made a clicking sound with his teeth. "You should also check out our neighbor Rich Copeland."

The sheriff turned to Brody with a raised brow, and Brody explained Copeland's attempts to dissuade them from opening the ranch.

The sheriff scribbled his name in his notepad. "I'll definitely look into him."

A weariness settled over Rachel. "Can I take Kenny home now? He's exhausted."

The sheriff nodded. "Sure. But if you think of anything else, ma'am, please give me a call."

Rachel's heart thudded with fear, but she agreed.

"I'll walk them home." Johnny gestured for her to lead the way, then he followed and picked Kenny up and carried him back to the cabin.

Kenny nuzzled against him, his eyes heavy.

Johnny patted his back. "In the morning, counselors are going to teach you how to tie ropes for the calf roping competition."

Kenny sighed sleepily but rallied with a smile. "Then I'll be a real cowboy?"

"Yes, buddy," Johnny said hugging him. "Then you'll be a real cowboy."

The hope in Kenny's tone only deepened Rachel's turmoil over the possibility of leaving.

They reached the cabin, and she climbed the steps, a sense of sadness overcoming her at the sight of the bird feeders and wind chimes hanging from the porch. The ranch felt like home.

Johnny took the key and unlocked the door, and fatigue pulled at Rachel. All she wanted to do was crawl into bed and forget what had happened in the dining hall. Forget about that man Burgess and Rex.

Tears burned her eyes, but she blinked them away and ushered Kenny inside.

"Let's take a quick bath to wash off that smoky odor," Rachel said. "Then it's bedtime."

Kenny nodded and he hurried into the bathroom. He liked his privacy now, so she and Johnny left him to wash up.

"Why don't you clean up, too," Johnny said as they stepped into the hall. "I'll wait out here."

"That's not necessary," Rachel said. "We're fine now. You can go."

He stroked her arm, his voice low, soothing. "I'm not leaving you tonight."

Johnny's gaze drifted down to her mouth, and her lips tingled as memories of that kiss flashed in her head.

She wanted to kiss him again. To have him hold her and make her forget that she and Kenny had almost died.

But she couldn't. So she left him to make sure Kenny was out of the bath and tucked into bed before she took a shower.

And as much as she wanted Johnny to join her, she would do it alone.

JOHNNY LISTENED TO RACHEL tuck Kenny into bed, then heard the shower running and groaned as he imagined Rachel stripping and climbing beneath the spray of water. She was only a room away, naked, wet, so beautiful.

Yet she was scared and still harboring secrets.

He wanted to push her for more answers. But God help him, he also wanted to join her. To taste her lips again and erase the terror that had gripped him when he'd realized she was trapped in that burning building.

He paced the cabin, struggling to maintain control. Finally, the water kicked off, and he imagined her slipping on some sexy pajamas.

A few minutes later, she stepped into the den.

Her hair lay across her shoulders in exotic waves, making his fingers itch to touch the silky strands. The scent of her body wash floated to him, a soft sensual fragrance that stirred his desires.

Then need darkened her eyes, and Johnny was lost.

"God, Rachel…" He strode toward her and wrapped his fingers around her arms. "Talk to me. Please."

"I don't want to talk," she said softly.

Johnny searched her face. He'd fallen for the wrong woman once before and been burned badly.

And Rachel was keeping secrets.

But his reservations faded when hunger echoed in her soft husky sigh.

He licked his lips. "What do you want, Rachel?"

Her chest rose and fell with a strained breath. "I want you to kiss me."

Chapter Thirteen

Johnny knew he should resist Rachel, but her admission aroused every male need in his body. The aching hunger he'd felt ever since that first kiss had been hammering away at his self-control for days.

Knowing she wanted him, that she needed him, ignited a fire in his belly.

"Rachel—"

She shushed him by placing a finger over his lips. His heart drummed in his chest. His breath quickened.

Images of her terrified face when he'd opened that pantry door flashed in his mind. She could have died, and he would have lost the opportunity to kiss her again.

Passion drove him to lift her finger from his lips and kiss it gently. Then he sucked on her fingertip, mesmerized at the sharp flash of pleasure that lit her eyes.

He wanted to give her more pleasure. To watch

her smile and writhe beneath him, to have those legs wrapped around his waist while he pumped inside her, to hear her whisper his name as she came in a mind-numbing climax.

But remembering she was skittish, he moved slowly, tucked a strand of her damp hair behind one delicate ear, then cupped her face between his hands and planted his mouth over hers. The kiss started out gentle, but need and hunger engulfed him, and he teased her lips apart, then plunged his tongue inside.

Her low, throaty moan spurred him on, and he deepened the kiss, his sex hardening as she slipped off his Stetson, tossed it to the chair by the fireplace, then threaded her fingers into his hair. One hand snaked down to untie the belt of her robe and it fell open, exposing the soft pajamas she wore beneath.

He wanted her naked. With nothing between them but skin and sweat and passion.

Trailing kisses along her throat and jaw, he unbuttoned the top button of the pajama top, parting the fabric to reveal her bare breasts. The dark tips of her nipples stiffened beneath his perusal, making his mouth water for a taste.

"Johnny…"

His fingers brushed lovingly over one turgid peak and he glanced up through a haze of desire. Her eyes looked glazed with need, as well, and her fingers stroked his hair from his forehead in a feminine gesture that spiked his blood.

He couldn't wait any longer. He pulled her up against him and closed his mouth over one nipple. She moaned and leaned into him, throwing her head back in submission, and he suckled her, laving one breast, then the other until her legs buckled.

He caught her around the waist, his breathing raspy as he walked her backward toward the sofa. She clung to him, rubbing herself against him as he lowered her to the cushions. Then she dragged his face toward her and kissed him, deep, bold, intense, as if she was as starved for him as he was for her.

Johnny had had his share of lovers, teenagers when he was younger, rodeo groupies in his twenties, but never anyone he cared about.

Rachel was different. Her touch triggered emotions he'd never felt before. He didn't just want sex with Rachel.

He wanted to make love to her.

His throat convulsed. Where had that thought come from?

Johnny Long had never *made love* to any woman. And the last one he'd had sex with had screwed him, both literally and figuratively.

But this was Rachel, not Gwen.

Still, Rachel was keeping secrets from him....

Then she raked her foot along his leg and he forgot about secrets and questions and doubts, and savored the feel of her skin against his and the sultry way she undulated beneath him.

He stroked her crotch with his sex, his breathing ragged as his erection thickened to a painful ache, then he inched his hands down to strip her pajama pants. One inch, two, he imagined her elation as he parted her legs and tasted her sweetness, but his fingers brushed over a puckered scar above her hipbone, and she tensed.

Johnny lowered the waistband, wanting to see more, needing to know how she'd gotten that scar, but she grabbed his shoulders and pushed at him.

"Stop, Johnny...stop."

He froze, then glanced into her eyes and saw fear, and his stomach knotted.

Their gazes locked as he eased his body away from her. A charged tension rippled between them, and he feasted on her beautiful heavy breasts, the tips pink from his loving. He wanted to touch her again, to take her back to that moment when they'd both been drugged with pleasure.

But the pain in her eyes sobered him.

"Who hurt you, Rachel?"

Her breath caught, and she shook her head in denial, then hastily began buttoning her pajamas. Her fingers were shaking, and he reached out to help her, but she paced to the fireplace, and turned her back to him. "Please, Johnny, just go."

"No."

She whirled around, panic and anger flashing in her expression. She reminded him of a wounded animal caught in a trap.

But he refused to leave tonight. He wanted her to talk to him.

And even if she didn't, she might be in danger. He'd stay with her around the clock.

If someone tried to hurt her, they'd have to go through him first.

RACHEL SHOULD NEVER have let Johnny get so close. And she shouldn't have allowed him to touch her.

But she had craved his comfort and his kiss.

Only the moment he'd seen that scar, her fight-and-flee instincts had kicked in, and she'd tensed.

"Rachel?" Johnny said in a husky whisper. "Tell me who it was."

She squared her shoulders. "I can't discuss my past."

Frustration lined Johnny's face. "Dammit, I'm trying to help you, to protect you." Johnny folded his arms, then lowered his voice to a husky whisper. "Now tell me. Was it your boyfriend? Lover? Husband?"

Her throat clogged with emotions. She wanted to trust him so badly that tears burned her eyes.

She was so tired of being alone. Of running. Of never leaning on anyone.

She wanted to lean on him. "My ex."

A muscle ticked in his jaw. "Kenny's father?"

A brief nod was all she could manage.

His dark eyes probed her. "Where is he now?"

"I don't know," Rachel said honestly. "The last time I saw him was in Phoenix."

"When was that?"

Rachel's pulse throbbed. "A couple of weeks ago."

A long tense second passed. "You've been moving around to keep him from finding you?"

Pain wrenched her heart. "Yes."

Another heartbeat of silence. This one so intense that Rachel feared she'd made a mistake and confess the truth. At least the portion of it she was willing to share.

Johnny's gaze moved over her, reminding her that they'd been nearly naked only moments before and that she still wanted him.

And she hadn't wanted a man since Rex.

Johnny cleared his throat. "Do you think your ex set that fire tonight?"

Rachel mentally debated the question just as she had ever since she and Kenny had gotten trapped in the pantry. "I don't know. Maybe." Her throat felt tight. "But I don't think he would hurt Kenny. He keeps saying that he wants his son."

"But you don't want him to be with Kenny because he's violent?"

"He never hit Kenny," she whispered, not in defense of the man, but because she would have killed him herself if he had. "But he liked control, and I refused to let my son be raised in an abusive environment, verbal or physical."

His voice softened. "That's understandable."

Self-recriminations screamed in her head. "I know what you're thinking. That I was stupid to get involved with him in the first place. That it was my fault."

"That's not what I was thinking at all, Rachel." Johnny shook his head, a lock of his dark hair falling across his forehead. Rachel could barely resist reaching out to brush it back. She'd never cared what anyone thought before, but now she desperately wanted Johnny to see her as a good mother, as a desirable woman, not as a pathetic, weak fool.

"I'd like to erase the pain he caused you." Johnny closed the distance between them, lifted her hand in his and gently traced his finger over her palm.

Rachel licked her lips, struggling to breathe. "You can't."

"Maybe I can," he said in a gruff whisper. "But you have to let me in. I understand exactly what it's like to have a father beat up on you. And I know how easy it is to fall for someone's charms and miss seeing they have their own agenda."

Rachel remembered the publicity about him and the hint of sexual charges that he'd firmly denied. "The woman in the paper?"

A sound of disgust rumbled from his throat. "Yes. Her name was Gwen. She made claims…"

"That you drugged her to seduce her," Rachel filled in.

Anguish deepened the grooves around Johnny's eyes, and for the first time in ages, Rachel forgot about her own problems in the wake of her compassion for him. "For what it's worth, Johnny, I don't believe those charges."

His tormented gaze searched hers. "Why not? Because I donated money to the ranch?" He shrugged. "Some folks would say I'm only volunteering at the BBL as a way to redeem my reputation."

Rachel curled her fingers into his hand. "They're wrong. You've not only been patient with Kenny, but you've been good to all the boys and to me."

She could easily see how a desperate, troubled woman would use Johnny. Maybe even stalk him as Rex had stalked her. "You're dedicated and kind and a wonderful role model."

He'd been firm but fair when that teenaged boy had pulled the prank on her. And from what she'd heard in the dining hall, he hadn't threatened violence or used his fists, or even cursed.

All things Rex would have done.

Emotions flickered across Johnny's face, and Rachel's heart melted. At one time Johnny might have been the arrogant, cocky rodeo star some of the media had portrayed him to be. But he had changed.

And he didn't deserve to be hurt because of her problems.

JOHNNY'S HEART TWISTED at Rachel's words. How long had it been since anyone had really believed in him? Not his old man, for sure. And he barely remembered his mother.

She hadn't wanted him. And his daddy had beat the hell out of him every chance he'd gotten.

By the time he was five, Johnny had known he was no good.

So he'd purged his anger through adrenaline rushes. Roping calves. Bareback riding. Breaking wild horses. On the back of a bull.

And he'd been good at it. Hell, he hadn't cared if he lived or died. He'd just needed the high to ease the pain of not being loved.

But when he'd first achieved fame, he'd mistaken women throwing themselves at him for love. For true affection.

Then he'd realized they were just infatuated with the rodeo star.

Not the real man.

Could Rachel see beneath the surface and really love him for the man he wanted to be?

"Johnny," Rachel said, "if you're worried about my ex finding me and endangering the other boys, Kenny and I will leave in the morning."

"I don't want you to go." He couldn't let the first woman he'd cared for in years walk away.

"But—"

"We don't know for sure he did it. There's Burgess and Copeland, too. They both have motive." Johnny hesitated. "Meanwhile, Brody's hiring extra security," Johnny said. "Do you have a photo of your ex I can give to security so they'll know how to spot him?"

"No," Rachel said frantically.

"Then give me his name and a description."

"I can't do this…"

Johnny frowned. "Why are you protecting him? If he set that fire, he should go to jail."

"I'm not protecting him, I'm protecting Kenny." Rachel clutched his hand, her tone frantic. "He has money. He knows people, has expensive lawyers and cops in his pocket. And I saw an article in the paper today where the judge who granted me the divorce was murdered. I think he did it."

"Then you have to go to the police, Rachel."

She shook her head wildly. "No. Even if he is arrested, he'll be out in a day and then he'll be even more angry and determined to kill me."

"I won't let him get to you and Kenny." A vein bulged in Johnny's jaw. "What is his name?"

Rachel took a deep breath. He thought she wasn't going to answer, but finally she whispered the word "Rex."

"Rex Simmons?"

She stared at him for a long moment as if debating the answer, then shook her head. "Rodgers."

Johnny's chest swelled. She'd trusted him. And for Rachel, her trust was the most precious gift she could give him.

"But please don't call the sheriff," Rachel pleaded.

Johnny hesitated. If this Rex guy did have someone in his pocket… "All right, but if he shows up and we discover he set the fire, I'll have to turn him in. We can't let him endanger anyone here."

"Of course not." She closed her eyes for a moment, then opened them and gave him a pained look that twisted his heart. "Thank you, Johnny. I just want to protect my son."

Johnny pulled her into his arms and rubbed her back. "Don't worry, he won't hurt you or Kenny, Rachel. Not as long as I'm around."

She sagged against him, and Johnny held her

close. He wanted to take her to bed, to comfort her all night. To make love to her until he erased all the memories of her ex.

But he wouldn't push her or try to own her like her husband had. Because he couldn't stand the thought of losing her or her son now. And trying to control or force her would send her running.

RACHEL'S RUNNING DAYS were about to come to an end.

So were her days of whoring around.

Rex bit the inside of his cheek so hard that he tasted blood, his gaze trained on the cabin where he'd seen that rodeo guy with Rachel and his little boy.

Johnny Long was in there now. What was the son of a bitch doing? Ramming himself inside her like some animal?

The thought made nausea climb his throat. He stroked the butt of his gun, anxious to make the man suffer.

But dammit, the cops had been crawling all over the place tonight. The cops and the fire chief.

It was too dangerous.

He wanted them to pay, and they would, but Rex Presley didn't intend to go to jail for serving justice.

No, he wouldn't get caught. He was too smart.

He glanced down at the news article about the

upcoming rodeo at the BBL, a rodeo starring the one and only Johnny Long.

The rodeo would be the perfect place to strike. There would be hundreds of people around. Strangers. Kids. Families.

It would be easy to blend in.

Then he'd find a way to kill Johnny Long and his cheating wife and take his son with him when he left.

Chapter Fourteen

Guilt pressed heavily against Rachel's heart as she slipped into her bedroom and closed the door. Johnny had been so good to her and Kenny, had protected them, had saved their lives. He was even going to sleep on her couch to make sure she felt safe tonight.

But she'd just lied to him about Rex's name.

Tears filled her eyes, and she rushed into the bathroom, buried her face into a towel and let the tears fall. Tears for the mistakes she'd made by marrying Rex. Tears for the life her son had had to lead. Tears of frustration that she didn't know how to change her situation and give Kenny a better future.

If she confided Rex's real name to Johnny, he'd inform the sheriff, then he'd learn about the warrant. Rex had so many people in his pocket that she'd go to jail and rot in a cell while Rex took Kenny.

Rex had turned his rage on her. It would only be a matter of time before he turned it on her son.

She wished she'd never come here.

Being on the ranch with these loving people made her realize just how lonely she was. Just how nerve-racking and miserable living on the run had become.

Worse, she'd seen how much Kenny had missed out by not having a real home or a father. By not being able to lead a normal, stable life.

By having to live without friends, and having to lie to the ones he did make.

Then having to leave them over and over again.

Her tears fell harder, and she smothered the sound, but a sense of hopelessness filled her. She wanted to stay here with Kenny and let him be a cowboy and learn to ride and be in the rodeo.

And she wanted to be whole again. To not cower or run away if a man touched her. Damn Rex for doing that to her.

Johnny's touches had been demanding but gentle. Hungry but sensual. Physically titillating yet emotionally arousing, as well.

For the first time since Rex, she really yearned to be with a man. And he was just a room away....

She ached to share her problems, confess the truth, let him comfort her. And she wanted to comfort him.

She wanted his hands on her, his lips on her;

she wanted to make love to him. And with Johnny, she sensed it *would* be making love.

Not like the rough, awkward, forced sex with Rex.

Suddenly exhausted, she dried her eyes, blew her nose, then stared at herself in the mirror. Once upon a time, she'd considered herself a smart woman. She'd had aspirations. Career goals.

Then her parents had died and she'd been grief-stricken and lost and fallen for Rex's charms.

She had made such a mess of her life.

Frustrated, she pressed her hand to her mouth to stifle another cry. She had to figure out a way to stop Rex from coming after her and Kenny.

But short of killing the man herself, she didn't know how that was possible.

Besides, at one time she'd considered nursing, helping people. She was not a killer.

If he hurt Kenny, you could do it.

Yes, she had no doubt about that. But she didn't intend to give him the opportunity.

A headache pulsed behind her eyes, and she crawled into bed, pulled the covers over her and closed her eyes. Johnny was only a few feet away; she could sleep knowing she and her son were safe for at least tonight.

Johnny said that Brody was hiring extra security. If Rex showed up, they'd catch him.

But even as she tried to fall asleep, the scent of

Rex's cologne haunted her and she couldn't totally relax. Her ex was cunning enough to sneak past whatever extra security Brody hired. Was mean enough to hurt anyone to get to her.

Was slick enough to charm his way past reporters and judges and make her look like an unfit mother.

And she couldn't stand for Kenny—or Johnny—to see her like that.

JOHNNY REMOVED HIS STETSON and boots and stretched out on the sofa, his mind ticking over the conversation with Rachel.

He wished to hell he could fix her problems. Wished she didn't have an ex who still obviously wanted her, and that the bastard had never hurt her.

Because he wanted her with a vengeance himself. Her lips, her body, her husky sigh had made him feel more potently sexy than he'd felt in years. Maybe ever.

But he wanted more than sex. He wanted to make her happy, to take care of her…

He lurched to a sitting position, shocked at that thought. Johnny Long had been a rodeo playboy.

It didn't take a rocket scientist to figure out that his lifestyle had been a facade to make up for the bad childhood and the low self-esteem his sorry daddy had pounded into him as a kid. No, he'd done some major soul searching after the incident with Gwen and figured all that out on his own. The girls, the money, the victories, the glory...all to try to fill the void he'd felt growing up.

All to seek approval.

But it had backfired in the end.

Rachel was the real deal. He didn't want her as a trophy girl or to add her to the notches on his bedpost.

He cared about her. She was sweet, vulnerable, beautiful and a devoted mother, and she stirred emotions that he'd never felt for another woman.

He needed more time to gain her trust and make her feel safe. But first, he had to find this bastard Rex and force him to disappear from her life.

He'd consult with Leon again. Instead of investigating Rachel, he'd ask him to track down her ex.

His mind made up, he finally closed his eyes and fell asleep.

But in the middle of the night, a noise startled him awake. He tensed and sat up, then automatically reached for his gun, but remembered he'd left it locked in his truck because of the kids on the ranch.

His heart pounding, he searched the darkness. The wind whistled outside. A sliver of moonlight wove its way through the sheer curtains, painting shadows along the walls of the den, and a tree branch scraped the window outside.

The noise sounded again. A low moan? A cry? A sob? Then a thud.

Kenny? Rachel?

He stood, scanning the room and listening for the direction of the noise.

Rachel's room.

Anger coiled inside him as he inched toward her room. If her ex had shown up, he'd catch him red-handed. And he'd beat him till the jerk swore he'd leave her alone.

Braced for a fight, he crept toward her room, then eased the door open just a fraction of an inch. Another low sob, a cry, echoed through the air.

He narrowed his eyes, squinting through the darkness, searching for an intruder, but there was no one inside.

No one except Rachel. She was twisting and turning on the bed, tangled in the covers, sobbing.

"Please, no, stop…don't hurt him…"

Johnny's throat thickened with compassion and anger. Shoulders tense, he strode into the room, then lowered himself on the bed beside her. Knowing she was in the midst of a nightmare, he gently brushed her hair away from her cheek, but it was damp from her tears, and through the moonlight bathing her face, he noticed her eyes were red and puffy.

His stomach clenched. Johnny Long had always been a sucker for a woman's tears. And this woman's were real.

Well aware she was in the midst of some horrid memory, he gently stroked her cheek. "Rachel?"

She rolled sideways, burying her face in the pillow as if she wanted to hide herself—or her tears.

What had that SOB done to her?

Using the pad of his thumb, he stroked her cheek again. "Rachel, shh, it's okay. You and Kenny are safe now."

She moaned, a gut-wrenching sound that shattered the last remnants of his restraint, and he stretched out on the mattress beside her and cradled her in his arms.

She opened her eyes for a brief moment and stared up at him, her slender body quivering against him. Her gaze looked foggy, confused, tormented. Then she seemed to register who he was and she clamped her teeth over her bottom lip.

"I'm sorry," she whispered. "I shouldn't have come here."

He stroked her back, rubbing slow soothing circles. "Shh, honey. Just go back to sleep. Everything's going to be all right."

She clutched his arms and buried her head against him, and he held her tight, savoring her sultry scent and sweetness. "I won't let anything hurt you or Kenny, Rachel. I promise."

She nodded against his chest, and finally relaxed and curled up against him.

Images of the two of them entwined after a long night of lovemaking stirred in his head. Maybe one day they could be together like that.

But tonight he'd be content to simply hold her.

RACHEL SLOWLY ROUSED from sleep, cocooned in Johnny's arms. His heady masculine scent permeated the air, obliterating memories of Rex's suffocating smell, and his strong arms and firm body wound around hers made her feel safe and loved.

Her pulse clamored, though, as reality set in.

Someone had set fire to the dining hall, and she and Kenny had almost died.

She snuggled against Johnny for another second, savoring the sanctity she'd found during the night. But she could not get used to Johnny taking care of her.

Rex would kill him to hurt her, and she couldn't live with his death on her conscience.

She slowly extricated herself from his embrace, but just as she slid to the edge of the mattress, Johnny caught her arm.

"Where are you going?"

Rachel sucked in a trembling breath, then faced him, her heart in her throat. "Kenny's in the other room. I...don't want him to find us in bed together."

Johnny's eyes flickered with a myriad of emotions she didn't understand. "Nothing happened, Rachel."

"I know," she said softly, although kissing Johnny had been more intimate and fulfilling than any sex with Rex had ever been. "But still..."

"I understand." He swung his legs over the side and stood, then looked at the grandfather clock against the far wall. "I need to get going, anyway."

"And I need to get dressed for work." The memory of the fire nagged at her, though. "What about the dining hall and kitchen? The damage won't force you to shut down?"

"We're not shutting down. The damage was contained to one area of the dining hall and the section of the kitchen near the pantry. Brody was going to have a cleanup crew work during the night." He eased himself toward the den door and she followed, her heart racing as he yanked on his boots and retrieved his Stetson.

Simply watching the big cowboy do those two things seemed somehow intimate and made her wonder what it would be like to wake up every morning with Johnny. They'd make love at night or maybe in the early hours of the morning before Kenny woke up, and she'd lie in his arms and feel his chest rising and falling against her own.

Oblivious to her thoughts, he continued, "We may have to cordon off that area of the dining hall, but hopefully the kitchen will be in working order. If we have to, there are picnic tables outside and the kids can eat there."

"That might be nice. Maybe Ms. Ellen and I can plan a picnic lunch menu."

Johnny smiled. "Sounds like a plan." He gestured toward Kenny's room. "You two gonna be okay this morning?"

Rachel nodded. "Thank you for…staying."

A frisson of hunger flashed in his eyes. "Thank you for trusting me."

Rachel's chest heaved as guilt once again assaulted her. She had turned into the very kind of person she despised—a liar.

She opened her mouth to confess everything. But Johnny's cell phone buzzed, and he snatched the phone. When he checked the caller ID, a low sound of disgust rumbled from his throat.

"Who is it?" Rachel asked.

"That damn reporter."

A drum beat inside Rachel's chest. The reporter would have questions about the fire. She had to ask Johnny for one more favor.

"What are you going to tell her?" Rachel asked.

Johnny's gaze met hers. "That the sheriff is investigating."

"I…don't want my name printed in the paper."

A series of emotions played across his face as he studied her. "Because your ex might see it and find you?"

She nodded.

"I'll take care of it."

Tears clogged Rachel's throat at Johnny's declaration. She wanted to thank him again, to ask him to come back to bed and make love to her.

To tell him that she loved him.

But the realization that she had fallen for Johnny terrified her.

Chapter Fifteen

Johnny hated to leave Rachel and Kenny for a moment. The fear that something would happen to them nagged at him. But it was daylight, Brody had hired extra security, Rachel had her cell phone and she would be with Ms. Ellen most of the day.

He climbed in his truck and zipped back to the main house for a quick shower, debating on whether to tell Brody about Rachel's ex, but he needed more information first.

By the time he came down the steps, he found Rich Copeland pacing the foyer. Copeland shot him an angry look.

"Where's Brody?"

"Probably at the dining hall getting ready to explain the fire we had last night to the staff and kids." Johnny crossed his arms and met him at the foot of the stairs. "You wouldn't happen to know anything about that, would you, Copeland?"

A vein bulged in the man's beefy neck. "You accusing me?"

Johnny forced himself to remain calm. Copeland reminded him of a bull about to charge. "You made it plain and clear that you opposed what we're doing here."

"I was worried about having a bunch of troubled hoodlums by my property," Copeland snapped. "And judging from my conversation with the sheriff, I was right. They are dangerous."

Johnny spoke through gritted teeth. "Or maybe you set that fire and you cut the fencing to sabotage our operation. You hoping bad publicity will shut us down?"

"Someone ought to shut you down," Copeland said sharply. "Before anyone gets hurt."

Johnny shoved his face in Copeland's. "No one had better get hurt," Johnny said. "And we are not shutting down. These boys need this ranch, and by God, I'm going to help Brody make it work."

"You'll be sorry," Copeland said.

Johnny crossed his arms. "Is that a threat?"

Copeland tilted his Stetson to the side. "No, a prediction. You invite trouble on your land, that's what you get. Trouble."

Copeland glared at him, then grabbed the door handle, opened it and stalked out. Johnny watched him go, anxiety knotting his stomach. What had made the man so cold?

Plagued with questions, he grabbed his hat, strode out the door and headed toward the dining hall. The sheriff was supposed to meet him and Brody this morning. Maybe he'd found evidence at the scene that would lead to the guilty party.

He met Brody at the dining hall and was amazed at the cleanup job. Other than the faint scent of smoke and the black walls in the far corner of the dining room and pantry area, the place was in decent shape.

"Copeland paid us a visit this morning," Johnny said.

Brody quirked his mouth sideways. "Let me guess. He confessed?"

"Right." Johnny gave a sarcastic laugh, then re-iterated the conversation to Brody.

Brody cursed. "If he did do this, he's going to jail."

The campers and staff began to file in, cutting off their speculations. Once the crew was seated with their plates, Brody explained about the arson while Johnny and the sheriff studied the group for anyone suspicious.

"I apologize for asking for alibis, but everyone on the ranch, staff and campers alike, have to be accounted for," Brody said. "Counselors, I need you to verify each camper's whereabouts at the time the fire broke out. And if anyone has seen anything suspicious or knows who's responsible for the fire and the fence being cut, please let us know."

Brody, Johnny and the sheriff divided up to question each of the staff members.

Frank Dunham, the man who'd known Carter, gave Johnny a wary look as he approached him. "You gonna try to pen this on me, too?"

Johnny shook his head. "We're just trying to get to the bottom of this. Rachel and her little boy were trapped in the pantry last night. They could have died."

Concern stretched across Dunham's face. "I didn't do it. I told you the reason I'm here. I would never hurt a woman or child."

"Have you seen anyone who looked suspicious?" Johnny asked. "Someone who looks as if he doesn't fit in?"

Dunham jammed his hands in his pockets. "You believe me?"

Johnny's gut told him the man was sincere. "Yeah, I do," Johnny said. "Now, have you heard any of the men or boys joking or bragging about cutting the fence or setting that fire?"

Dunham pursed his mouth in thought, then suddenly snapped his fingers. "Haven't heard anything, but I did see a car I thought looked odd. Out of place."

"Why? What kind of car was it?"

"One of those fancy Lincolns, you know a big black one. Not something any of the hands drive."

"Or the counselors," Johnny said in agreement.

Most of them had SUVs or trucks. And the young counselors couldn't afford an expensive town car.

"Thanks, Dunham. That might help."

Dunham nodded, then walked away and Johnny clenched his jaw.

A big fancy Lincoln town car. If Rachel's ex had money as she'd claimed, it sounded like the kind of vehicle he'd drive.

He walked outside, then punched in Leon's number. The man's voice mail picked up, and Johnny left a message asking him to track down Rex Rodgers and find out what make of car he was driving.

If he'd set that fire, Johnny would find the bastard and make him pay.

Then he looked up and spotted Copeland talking to June Warner and knew they had other problems. Copeland was determined to make him and the ranch look bad.

He had to figure out a way to stop him.

RACHEL BUSIED HERSELF cleaning up the breakfast dishes, trying to distract herself from worrying. She had seen Johnny, Brody and the sheriff questioning the staff and had prayed they would find the arsonist.

That it wasn't Rex.

She didn't want to leave the BBL.

Or Johnny.

"I still can't believe someone tried to burn down the dining hall." Ms. Ellen's cheeks paled with worry. "I feel bad you and Kenny were here by yourself. I shouldn't have left you alone."

Rachel hugged the older woman. In spite of her attempt to keep her distance, she'd grown fond of her. "I'm glad you weren't here. You could have been hurt."

Ms. Ellen hugged her in return. "Still…it's horrible that someone would do such a thing."

Rachel wrung her hands on the dishcloth. "I know. I hope it doesn't affect the rodeo."

They finished cleaning up, but the scent of lingering smoke served as a constant reminder of the horror the night before. Riddled with tension, she decided to go and watch the boys practice.

But as she crossed the field toward the stables, she kept an eye out, scanning the pasture, the barn, looking for signs that Rex was watching her.

She passed Kim just before she reached the pens, and Kim rushed to her. "Rachel, I heard about last night. That must have been terrifying. Are you all right?"

She hated lying to these nice people.

"It was scary, but Johnny saved me and Kenny just in time."

Kim rubbed her arm. "That's Johnny for you. I just hope the sheriff figures out who did it."

"Me, too." Rachel couldn't stand to look into

her trusting eyes any longer. "Well, I'd better hurry. I don't want to miss Kenny's lesson."

She pasted on a smile, then hurried toward the stables. The boys practiced roping, had a riding lesson, and took a break to play a game of horseshoe and help set up the information booth for guests to pick up packets about the ranch's services and camps.

Other vendors arrived with their booths to set up, meeting with Brody to discuss locations and details. When the boys broke from their last session, Kenny ran over to hug her.

"We're gonna ride out by the stream," Kenny said. "And go fishing!"

Rachel ruffled his hair and smiled. "Have fun. I'll see you at dinner."

Kenny raced off to join the counselor and his group, and Rachel headed back to her cabin to rest a few minutes before the dinner rush.

But the moment she stepped inside the cabin, the hairs on the back of her neck prickled. That scent…the cologne…was she imagining it?

She peered inside the den, but saw nothing amiss, then eased her way toward the bedroom. Nausea flooded her throat as her gaze fell on her bed.

A black rose lay on her pillow.

Rex was here.

Panic robbed her breath. She had to find Kenny

and make sure he was okay. If Rex took Kenny while he was out fishing, they'd disappear and she'd never see him again.

JOHNNY HIGH-FIVED THE last group as he gave them tips on controlling their horse and maneuvering the barrels for the barrel-race competition.

June Warner and her cameraman were watching, taking candid shots for promotional purposes.

Excitement fueled Johnny. The show would go on.

Then he'd return to his own spread. He just hoped they impressed the fans and investors with their mission, and that he left Brody with enough financial backing to keep the ranch afoot for the next few years.

When he looked up, June waved to him. "Johnny, is it true there was a fire last night in the dining hall? That it was arson?"

Johnny silently cursed. This conversation was unavoidable, but he had to reassure the public. "At this point, we're not certain what happened. The sheriff is investigating the matter."

"Do you have any suspects?"

"As I said, the sheriff is handling the investigation. I'm certain he'll let us know what he finds."

"Do you think it's safe here for the boys?"

Johnny nodded. She'd obviously picked up the thread of Copeland's accusations. "We've hired extra security, and I've personally checked and rechecked safety precautions for all the events."

"So you are still planning to have the rodeo?"

"Absolutely." Johnny understood how to play the media game, and despite the fact that they had turned on him, he offered her his killer smile. "The investors and staff are dedicated to making this ranch work. I certainly could have used a place like this when I was growing up, and want to make sure that these boys receive the support and encouragement they need to become successful individuals and contributing members of society."

June's eyes flickered with mischief. "Care to comment on the past?"

Johnny gritted his teeth, but let his heart show through in his words. "Our motto is that everyone deserves a second chance. Who better to prove that than a tired rodeo boy with a shady past himself?"

That earned a laugh as he'd hoped, and he waved off more questions. His cell phone buzzed, and he checked the caller ID box. Leon.

"Excuse me, I have to take this."

The reporter thanked him, then turned to interview Ricardo, who beamed beneath the attention. Maybe Ricardo was going to be one of their success stories.

Johnny walked to the main house and stepped

inside his office wanting privacy. His heart raced as he answered the call.

"Johnny Long."

"I looked into the ex-husband, like you asked." Johnny tensed. "And?"

"As you suspected, Simmons is not the woman's real name. It's Presley."

Johnny swallowed, a bad feeling pinching his gut. "Go on."

"Her husband's name was Rex, that part is true. But she lied about his last name, too. It wasn't Rodgers. It's Presley."

Disappointment knifed through Johnny. "What kind of car does he drive?"

"A black Lincoln town car."

Dammit. "Were there abuse charges filed against the ex? Had she gotten a restraining order?"

"No and no." The P.I. sighed. "As a matter of fact, there's a warrant out for Rachel Presley's arrest for the attempted murder of her husband, Rex, and for kidnapping their son."

The breath left Johnny's chest in a painful rush, and he stood and strode to the window. Not only had Rachel lied to him again, but he'd kept her secrets from Brody and the police, which meant he could be arrested as an accomplice.

Dammit. She was worse than Gwen.

She'd made him care about her while she'd only been using him to hide from the police.

RACHEL RACED OUTSIDE, panic setting in as she hurried toward the barn. The kids probably wouldn't be back for an hour. She'd wait.

But the camp minivan pulled up a few minutes later. Time ticked slowly by as the kids climbed off and she searched the faces for her son. But he didn't get off, and she ran over to the counselors.

Blair was on her cell phone, her expression strained.

Rachel caught her arm. "Where's Kenny?"

Blair closed her phone, her eyes wide with fear. "I…don't know what happened, Ms. Simmons. One minute he was there, and the next minute he was gone."

Rachel's world spun in a dizzying rush. Oh, God…Kenny was missing.

REX TOSSED DOWN A SCOTCH as he paced the hotel room. Why in the hell Rachel had chosen to live on some godforsaken nowhere ranch when he'd offered her a glitzy life on his arm was beyond him.

But the damn woman would not cut him out of her life.

No one rejected Rex Presley.

He was in charge, and dammit, he would get her back. Then he'd make her suffer for embarrassing him in front of his friends.

Yes, he'd make her suffer. Long and hard.

Before he was finished, she'd cry and beg him to take her back.

He'd have her on her knees in no time.

The scotch burned a path down his throat, and he poured a second shot, then downed it, smiling as its comforting warmth spread through him and he imagined all the ways he would torture her.

Then he'd teach his son how to be a real man, not some lame cowboy.

Chapter Sixteen

Johnny's boots hit the floor with a thud as he stood and strode to the door. He had to talk to Rachel.

And this time he'd find out why she'd played him for a fool.

Damn. If June Warner got wind of this tidbit, the publicity would destroy the ranch. All their good intentions would be lost.

Because he'd been an idiot over a woman again.

No wonder Rachel had avoided the reporter. And the sheriff. No wonder she'd been on the run.

It all made sense now. Her nervous behavior. Kenny's frightened looks when they'd first arrived.

Had she played him from the beginning? Given him just enough tears and vulnerable looks that he'd fallen into her cunning hands?

But what about those bruises? And the fire? And the man who'd assaulted her in the barn? She hadn't made those things up. He had rescued her and Kenny himself.

A self-disgusted groan rolled from his gut.

His cell phone buzzed, and he descended the front porch steps and climbed in his truck, checking the caller ID box as he started the engine. Rachel.

Fury simmered through his blood, and he hesitated. He didn't intend to confront her over the phone and give her time to escape.

This time he wouldn't fall for her act.

Forcing his voice to remain calm, he connected the call. "Hello."

"Johnny." Her voice sounded screechy, panicked. "Kenny's missing!"

Despite his anger, her words sent a streak of fear through him. "What?"

"He's missing," Rachel cried.

Was that real terror in her voice? It sounded sincere and made his throat close. But he reined in his emotions, determined not to be played again. "What happened?"

A muffled sound echoed over the line, then her shaky breath. "Kenny's group went to the creek to fish, but they came back early because Kenny disappeared. Blair's already called Brody."

Johnny felt as if he'd been punched in the gut. If Kenny had gone missing while under the counselor's supervision, Rachel wasn't making it up.

"Please, Johnny." Rachel's voice broke on another sob. "We have to find him. I can't let Rex take him away… There's no telling what he'd do to h-him."

Johnny's anger took a backseat to fear. Even if Rachel had lied to him, she loved that boy dearly.

"Don't panic," Johnny said. "He probably just wandered off. Maybe he was chasing a rabbit or saw something in the woods he wanted to explore."

A gut-wrenching sob tore from her and ripped out Johnny's heart.

He had to clear his throat to speak. "I'll be right there." He gunned the engine, sending dirt flying from his tires as he sped toward the stable. "We'll find him, I promise."

His heart pounded as he hightailed it over the hill to the stable. His phone buzzed again and he snatched it up.

"Johnny, Blair called—"

"I know, Kenny's missing," Johnny said. "I just talked to Rachel."

"On foot he couldn't have gotten very far. I'll organize a search party."

"Thanks. I'm on my way to meet Rachel."

A bead of perspiration trickled down Johnny's neck as he noticed the sun sinking lower into the sky. Even if Kenny had just wandered off on his own, there were hundreds of acres to search, and the temperature could get chilly at night. There were also coyotes and snakes and other dangers for a young boy on the land.

But what if Rachel was right? What if her ex had kidnapped Kenny?

If he was driving, he could already be off the ranch and miles away by now.

"I'M SO SORRY, MS. SIMMONS," Blair said, her voice quivering. "I just turned my head for a minute and he was gone."

Rachel's emotions ping-ponged between blaming the young girl and sympathy.

If Rex had Kenny, it was her fault. Her fault for marrying him. If she'd warned Blair about her ex, the girl would have kept a closer eye on him.

"Let's just focus on finding him." Rachel searched the boys' faces. "Did any of you guys see what happened?"

The group of six- and seven-year-olds looked worried and confused, but none of them spoke up.

One of the boys shrugged. "Maybe he fell in the water."

Rachel's heart churned at that thought.

Blair fiddled with the pocket of her jean jacket. "Don't worry, Ms. Simmons, that's the first place we looked, and the water's not that deep where we were."

Rachel wanted to scream that children had drowned in bathtubs before, but bit her tongue and silently vowed to give Kenny swimming lessons once he was back safe with her.

Johnny's pickup roared up, and he jumped out and jogged toward her.

"Johnny, we have to do something." Rachel clenched his arms and lowered her voice to a pained whisper. "If Rex has him, I'll never see him again."

"Would Kenny willingly go with your ex?"

Rachel shook her head. "No, he's terrified of him."

Johnny's jaw clenched. "I talked to Brody. He's gathering the ranch hands to look for him now."

"I'm so sorry, Mr. J." A tear rolled down Blair's cheek. "The boys were so excited about the fishing trip that they were running around and skipping stones in the creek while Andy and I unloaded the fishing gear. When I called the group together, Kenny was gone."

A dozen scenarios trolled through Johnny's mind. None of them good.

"We immediately searched the creek and the area," Blair said. "But we didn't see him, so we came back here."

The kids were huddled beneath a tree now, talking and playing with sticks in the dirt.

"How long did you wait before calling Brody?"

"Just a few minutes. Five, ten maybe." Blair

swiped at her tears, sounding contrite. "I should have called sooner..."

"It's all right, Blair," Johnny said in a gentle tone. "Brody's organizing a search party, and I'm going to hunt for him now." He gestured toward the boys. "Take the kids back to their cabin and stay with them."

Blair wiped at her eyes. "But I want to help search."

"No," Johnny said. "One boy is already missing. We don't want any more to wander off. That means every counselor needs to be on his toes and every camper accounted for."

Blair nodded. "Yes, sir, of course. I'll let the other counselors know." She hurried and ushered her group into the minivan.

Rachel followed him into the barn. "I'm going with you."

Johnny threw a stern look over his shoulder as he reached for a saddle and bridle. "Go back to the cabin and wait, Rachel. Maybe Kenny will show up there."

Rachel remembered the black rose and shivered. "No...I have to do something, look for him. I'm going with you."

Johnny began to saddle Soldier. "I said no. Now do as I said. Kenny might be at your cabin now."

"He's not," Rachel whispered hoarsely. "Rex is

on the ranch, Johnny. I know. He left a black rose on my bed."

Johnny narrowed his eyes. "A black rose?"

She nodded, her heart in her throat. "When I left Rex, he used to taunt me with black roses. He'd leave them everywhere. Crushed, dead rose petals to remind me that if he found me, he'd kill me."

RACHEL'S WORDS ECHOED in Johnny's head. *Her ex-husband left dead rose petals to remind her that he'd kill her.*

Was Rachel lying again as a ploy to gain his attention? Had her ex threatened to kill her?

If so, Kenny might be in serious danger.

He tightened the bridle on the horse and adjusted the saddle. He wanted to blast her for putting him and Brody in a bad position.

But first they had to find her son.

Time was of the essence.

Rachel grabbed a saddle and threw it over a dark brown gelding, and Johnny sighed and went to help her.

"I can do it."

"This is not a power struggle," Johnny said. "It'll be dark soon and I'm faster. We can't afford to waste a minute."

Anger flickered on her face, but she stepped

back, folded her arms and let him saddle the horse.

"You know how to ride?" Johnny asked as he helped her mount.

She nodded. "Don't worry about me. I'll keep up."

Johnny considered her point, and punched Brody's number. "Brody, I need you to have the security detail and staff ride around the ranch looking for any cars that don't belong."

"What are you getting at?" Brody asked. "You think someone kidnapped the boy?"

"It's possible the boy's father did," Johnny said. "Have security look for a black Lincoln town car."

Brody cleared his throat. "So this is a custody issue?"

"Maybe."

"Is this guy dangerous?"

"Rachel claims he is," Johnny said.

Brody huffed. "And you didn't think I needed to know about this before now?"

Johnny clenched the phone. "I'll explain later. Let's just find the boy first. Rachel and I are saddling up to ride out and look around."

For a moment, they discussed dividing up the search areas into quadrants, then Johnny hung up.

"Are you sure we don't need to take the truck?" Rachel asked.

"The security team will handle searching the

roads. Besides, a horse can go where a truck can't," Johnny said. "If Kenny did wander off or if he saw your ex, he might be hiding somewhere."

They mounted the horses and rode toward the eastern pasture where the creek ran. Several barns had been built on that side to house more quarter horses as they expanded the operation but were empty now. They would be the perfect place for a little boy to hide.

Maybe Rachel's ex had been hiding there, as well.

Johnny led the way, sending his stallion into a gallop, and Rachel followed behind, the wind whistling from the hills as they crossed the ranch. The sun had dipped below the trees now streaking the horizon in hazy red, yellow and orange lines, and the temperature was dropping, the sounds of night animals bursting to life.

An image of Kenny, so small, scared, running from his abusive father, or even lost and hungry, fending off a snake or coyote, made his skin crawl. The horses kicked dirt as their hooves skidded along the graveled path near the stream, and he and Rachel began to call out Kenny's name.

"Kenny, it's Mommy," Rachel shouted. "Honey, where are you?"

Johnny cupped his hand around his mouth. "If you can hear us, let us know where you are!"

They rode along the creek, checking for Kenny,

and Johnny guided his horse to a stop, tied his reins to a tree and used a flashlight to search along the bank for footprints while Rachel rode farther down and then circled back.

"Did you see anything?" she asked, her voice raw with nerves.

"No. You?"

Rachel shook her head, a tear rolling down her face. "What if we don't find him, Johnny? What if Rex has him and I never see him again?"

Johnny's heart tugged at the anguish in her voice. He wanted to assure her that they would find Kenny.

But if Rex had stolen the boy, he might be long gone by now.

Chapter Seventeen

Rachel shivered as night set in. What if Rex had Kenny and had already left the ranch?

No...she wouldn't give up.

"Kenny!" She guided the horse along behind Johnny as they rode through a wooded area. "Honey, where are you?"

Trees shook in the wind, cows mooed, and somewhere in the distance a wild mountain lion roared.

Her imagination drifted to all the dark things that could happen to a little boy on his own. This section of the ranch hadn't been developed yet, and the prospect of poisonous snakes and other wild animals posed dangers that could be deadly for her son. There were several ridges up ahead in the hilly part, ridges with sharp rocks and uneven land that dropped off several feet, drop-offs that Kenny might not see at night until it was too late. If he'd fallen, he could be lying at the bottom of a ravine, injured and needing help.

"Kenny!" Johnny shouted. "We're looking for you, son!"

Heavy gray clouds moved across the sky, the breeze stirring leaves behind her, and tree branches snapped with the force of the wind. Johnny steered his horse through the maze of trees, then to a clearing that led to a series of stables.

"I'll check the first barn while you look in the second," Rachel suggested.

Johnny shook his head. "No, we stay together. If your ex is dangerous like you claimed, he might have a gun."

A shudder coursed through Rachel. He was right.

Pebbles skidded beneath the horses' hooves as they galloped to the barn, slowed and climbed off. Johnny tied both of the animals to a post outside, then removed a handgun from his saddlebag and inched toward the first door.

"Stay behind me," Johnny ordered.

Rachel did as he said, practically hugging his back as they crept to the barn door. The wood squeaked as he eased the door open, and the fresh scent of hay hit Rachel. There were no animals housed here yet, and darkness shrouded the interior. Johnny shined a flashlight across the stalls as they searched.

"Kenny!" Johnny called.

They paused, listening for a sound, for Kenny's voice, any sign he was inside, but dead silence filled the air.

Johnny slipped to the next stall and looked inside while Rachel gravitated toward the back of the barn, willing her son to appear.

"If you're here, answer me, baby."

Seconds later, they'd searched the entire barn, and it was empty.

Disappointment warred with fear in Rachel's chest. "Come on, there's one more," Johnny said.

Rachel nodded, her throat aching too badly to speak. Outside, clouds covered the stars, and a clap of thunder rent the air. She checked the sky, growing more agitated as lightning flashed in jagged lines. What if Kenny was out in the open, the worst place to be in a storm?

"Rachel." Johnny squeezed her arm. "Come on, we're not giving up."

She stayed close beside him as they crossed to the second barn, both of them running when lightning crackled again, streaking the ground. When they reached the door, Johnny clenched his gun by his side and pushed open the door. Again, they were pitched in darkness, but she thought she heard a sound from somewhere in the back.

A rustling of hay? Maybe mice or a cat?

"Kenny," she said in a raw whisper. "Kenny, Mommy's here."

Another sound, feet moving across dirt? A whimper? Then one of the boards in a back stall banged.

Johnny motioned for her to stay behind him. She squeezed his arm to indicate she would, and they eased toward the sound. Another clap of thunder popped outside, lightning sending a shard of light across the back wall. Suddenly Rachel spotted the silhouette of a man lurching up and running toward the door.

"Kenny!" Rachel shouted.

A low cry, then a noise as if there was a scuffle.

Johnny took off running, wielding his gun at the ready. Rachel chased behind him, her instincts urging her on.

A screeching sound rent the air, then the back barn door whipped shut.

Johnny swung the flashlight toward the noise, his eyes widening. "Stay here."

Rachel's pulse pounded as Johnny dashed toward the back. But she couldn't just stand there. She ran behind him calling Kenny's name.

"Mommy!" Kenny yelled.

Just as she and Johnny made it to the back stall, the sound of horse hooves pounded the ground outside.

"Are you all right, Kenny?" Johnny asked. "Are you hurt?"

Kenny was huddled in the corner of the stall, hay sticking to his clothes and hair.

"That mean man tried to make me go with him," Kenny said in a shaky voice.

Johnny motioned Rachel toward her son. "Take him back to the cabin and let Brody know you found him! I'm going after the guy."

He disappeared through the door, and Rachel knelt and cupped Kenny's face between her hands. "Kenny, are you really okay?"

Kenny's head bobbed up and down. "I didn't want to go, Mommy!"

"I know, honey, I know, but it's okay now." Tears stung Rachel's eyes as she pulled her son into her arms.

JOHNNY JAMMED THE GUN into the back of his jeans as he mounted his horse, then snapped the reins and kicked the horse's sides, sending him into a gallop as he gave chase.

Thunder boomed and, on instinct, Soldier tried to buck and spin around to head back to the stables, but Johnny soothed him with a soft command, maintaining control by his grip on the reins. "Don't freak out on me now, boy," Johnny murmured. "We have to catch that bastard."

Soldier settled into the rhythm, and Johnny coaxed him to go faster as they crossed the pasture. The man was hightailing it, whipping the horse, dust flying behind him as he climbed the hill. On the other side of the ravine, the pasture banked up to a dirt road, where Johnny had a feeling the man had his car waiting.

He wouldn't let him get that far.

Nudging Soldier a little harder, he gripped the reins tighter and closed the distance. Judging from the awkward way the man sat in the saddle, he didn't ride much, which gave Johnny the advantage, and he quickly gained on him.

Obviously, the creep didn't know the lay of the land either, because he tried to steer the horse toward the ravine. A big mistake. The horse balked and skidded, fighting the man's commands, and Johnny dived from his horse and knocked the bastard to the ground.

They fought and rolled, tumbled down a hill, grunting and struggling. The man swung a fist up to connect with Johnny's jaw, and pain knifed through his cheek, but he punched the man in the gut, then his nose. Bones crunched, blood spurted and the man bellowed in pain.

"Damn you!"

A lightning bolt illuminated the man's face. Burgess.

"You son of a—" Johnny shoved the man to his back, then climbed on top of him, pulled his gun and jammed it in his face.

Fear made the whites of Burgess's eyes bulge,

and blood trickled down to his mouth. "Don't shoot," he cried. "Please…don't kill me."

Remembering the fear in Rachel's voice and Kenny's eyes a few moments earlier made it hard to restrain himself. He wanted to kill him.

"Please…" Burgess rasped. "I…don't want to die."

Johnny settled all his weight on the man, then jerked him by the collar, squeezing it so tight that Burgess gagged for a breath.

"Why did you try to kidnap the boy?"

"His father…" He coughed, sucking in blood.

Johnny pressed the tip of the gun into his temple. "What about him?"

"He…offered a reward," Burgess said hoarsely.

"For kidnapping his son?"

The man nodded. "And for bringing his wife back."

Johnny's heart drummed in his chest. "Where is he?"

"I don't know," Burgess said.

Johnny cocked the trigger. The click sounded ominous in the silence.

Burgess's shaky breath rattled with fear. "I swear I don't know where he is now."

"How did he contact you?"

Panic flashed in the man's eyes. "Friend of mine told me about it. He did some work for him before."

"You know he hit his wife?"

Guilt mingled with the panic on his face. "Listen, man, I just needed the money."

"So bad you'd turn a little boy and a woman over to an abusive man?"

"He's the kid's father. He's got rights."

"Not if he was abusing them he doesn't." Johnny waved the gun in front of Burgess's face and was rewarded by Burgess's eyes bulging with fear.

"You know, I could call the sheriff and have you arrested for kidnapping and assault on Rachel."

"I didn't assault her," Burgess argued. "I offered a deal, a trade-off."

Bile filled Johnny's throat. "What? You were going to let her go if she slept with you?"

Burgess's terrified look confirmed Johnny's suspicion.

"So, I'll just add arson and attempted murder to the kidnapping."

"I wasn't trying to kill them. I just wanted to smoke them out, but then you showed up."

"Damn good thing, too, or they might have died," Johnny spat back.

He should call McRae. But then he'd have to explain to the sheriff why he had been harboring a wanted woman.

He had to find out the truth first.

If Rachel had tried to kill her husband, she had

good reason. Maybe he had hit Kenny and killed that judge like she said, which meant the man was dangerous as hell.

His childhood memories haunted him. The very idea of a man beating on a woman and a child infuriated him, and he made a snap decision. "How much did he offer to pay you?"

Burgess stiffened. "Five grand."

Johnny cursed. "I'll double it." He pointed the gun at his forehead. "That is, if you disappear and never bother the woman or her son again."

"It's a deal," Burgess said in a strained voice.

Johnny squeezed his neck with one hand. "But if you contact Rachel's ex or ever set foot near them again, I promise you, I'll track you down." He narrowed his eyes to menacing slits. "And when I find you, and make no doubt that I *will* find you, I will put a bullet in your head."

Burgess nodded vigorously, and Johnny prayed he wasn't making a big mistake by letting the man go. But if he called the law on Burgess, he'd have to tell the sheriff the whole story, and that meant Rachel would be arrested and hauled to jail.

Then Rex would get Kenny.

And if Rex had paid someone to kidnap Kenny and drag Rachel back to him, he didn't deserve his son.

RACHEL ROCKED KENNY in her arms, grateful they'd found him in time and that he was safe.

"I didn't like him," Kenny whispered against her neck. "I wanted to beat him up and save you, Mommy."

Her heart ached. "I know, honey. I'm so sorry he scared you." She cupped his face between her hands. "And listen to me. I'm the mom here, the parent. I'm supposed to take care of you, not the other way around."

"But I'm the man of the house now." Kenny sniffed against her, and she wanted to find the brute and murder him for terrifying her son.

Rachel's heart broke for him. He was too young for such responsibility. How was she going to fix this?

For a moment, Kenny nestled up to her, his small body shaking, and Rachel held him, stroking his back and soothing him. Finally, when he seemed to calm, she pulled back to study him.

"Did he hurt you, Kenny?"

His chin quivered but he shook his head no.

"Thank God." She examined his arms and legs. "Do you know who he was?"

"No," Kenny said in a small voice. "He said he was taking me to Daddy."

Rachel bit back a scream of frustration. So Rex had hired some thug to kidnap her son. Probably to lure her into a trap so he could kill her.

That thought made her pulse pound, and she glanced around the barn again, searching the darkness in case Rex was close by. If he was watching, he'd know Johnny had chased after the man and she and Kenny were alone.

She clutched Kenny to her. "Come on, sweetie. We have to go."

Kenny tightened his grip around her neck. "Are we going away again?"

Rachel's throat closed on a sob. No, she didn't want to go, but she might not have a choice. A stranger had tried to kidnap her son. Brody and Johnny would want to tell the sheriff. Then he'd look into her marriage, and she'd go to jail…

Thunder boomed outside, rattling the barn roof, and the shrill wind whistled, snapping branches in its wake.

She slowed, checking each corner, listening for footsteps, her nerves on edge. Her gun was back at the cabin. If Rex attacked them here in the barn, she would be defenseless. He was strong, a bully who pounded his way to get control.

She had lost before. She wouldn't have a chance on her own. Not with him physically, or in court.

"Mom?" Kenny asked on another sniffle.

"Don't worry, buddy, I've got you now." She patted his back. "I have to let Brody know we found you. Everyone on the ranch has been searching for you."

Kenny pasted on a brave face, and she pulled away long enough to text Brody that they'd found Kenny so he would call off the search.

A second later, fierce protective instincts overcame her, and she clutched Kenny and made a run for her horse. Her gaze darted to the left and right, and she scanned the property surrounding the barn, searching for movement. She didn't allow herself to breathe until she'd mounted the horse and pulled Kenny up behind her.

"Hold tight." Rachel tugged Kenny's arms around her waist. Then she snapped the reins and yanked them to the right, commanding the horse to take them back to the cabin.

Thunderclouds rolled ominously across the sky, the path paved by streaks of lightning bouncing off the treetops. Kenny buried his head against her back, startling as each thunderclap boomed in the night. Raindrops began to splatter the ground, pelting them as the horse galloped across the pasture. She bypassed the dining hall, then slowed the horse to a trot as they approached the cabin.

Nerves tightened her stomach, and she scanned the front of the cabin and the surrounding property. What if Rex had hired the guy to kidnap Kenny so he could kill her while her son was gone?

Was he waiting in the cabin?

Chapter Eighteen

Rachel eased the horse to a stop a few feet from the cabin. She vaguely considered riding back to the barn and unsaddling him, but her first priority was to get Kenny safely inside. She and Johnny would deal with taking care of the animal later.

She climbed off, then peered around as she helped Kenny down and tied the horse to the post in the front. "Thanks for getting us back," she murmured as she patted his back.

Kenny still looked shaken, but he pulled her toward the barn. "We gots to feed Cleo and the pups."

Rachel wanted to argue, but Kenny loved the dogs so much that she didn't have the heart. He'd suffered enough trauma; maybe seeing the animals he loved would be therapeutic.

Still, she felt edgy as they went inside, but thankfully Johnny had told Kenny to leave a light on, and she instantly scanned the interior for Rex. Cleo and the puppies bounded up, licking and jumping all over Kenny, and he dropped to his knees and hugged them, rubbing their bellies.

Normally, Kenny fed the dogs and refilled the water bowls himself, but tonight she was anxious to tuck him into bed, so she handled those tasks while he petted the puppies.

"Where's Mr. J.?" Kenny asked.

"He'll be here soon," Rachel said. "Now let's go inside and put on our pj's."

Kenny hugged Cleo and the puppies one more time, then followed her back to the cabin.

Rachel held her breath as she unlocked the door. She immediately smelled Rex's cologne.

Remembering the black rose on her pillow, she flipped on a light, willing the cabin to be empty. If Rex was there, she just hoped she'd have time to reach her gun before he attacked.

Silence stole the air and accentuated the blustery sound of the brewing storm outside. Blinking at the brightness in the room, she visually scanned the corners. No Rex.

Clutching Kenny's hand, she inched into the hall and checked the bedrooms. Thankfully, they were empty, too.

Then she spotted a photo lying on Kenny's pillow and gasped.

It was a photo of the three of them on Christmas Day two years ago.

Kenny had been so excited over discovering his toys that morning when he'd run into the den that Rachel had faked her own happiness. But she'd been battered and sore, and hiding her bruises with powder so Kenny couldn't see the marks his father had made the night before.

Only Kenny had noticed and cried, and Rex had been furious and blamed her for spoiling their day.

Kenny's little body quivered as he stared at the photo, too. He obviously remembered that day, as well.

Even worse, Rex had cut her face from the picture as if he'd cut her from their lives.

As if she was dead and he and Kenny would move on without her.

JOHNNY HOPED TO HELL he'd done the right thing by paying off Burgess. His cell phone was buzzing as he watched the creep crawl in his SUV and drive away.

Johnny's phone buzzed again and he clicked to answer. "Johnny, it's Brody. Rachel left a message that you found the boy."

"Yeah," Johnny said, dreading the talk he had to have with his friend. "She's taken him back to the cabin."

"Where was he?"

"In one of the barns east of the stream." The phone crackled. "Listen, I'm breaking up. Just tell security to be on the watch for a black Lincoln town car or a dark blue SUV. If they spot either of those vehicles, I want to know."

"Johnny, what's going on?"

"I'll meet you in the morning and explain," Johnny said, stalling. "But right now, I need to check on Kenny and Rachel."

Brody hesitated, but seemed to accept his answer, which made him feel like a heel for not spilling his guts sooner. If someone got hurt because he'd kept quiet, he'd never forgive himself.

He ended the call, swung himself up in the saddle and nudged Soldier into a brisk gallop. As he rode, he kept his eyes trolling for trouble, for Burgess or Rex or some other creep who Rachel's ex might have sent on her tail.

Rain drizzled down, soaking his shirt, and he spotted her horse tied up outside. Lightning illuminated the cabin, and his pulse clamored as he searched for predators.

Soldier slowed and, on instinct, sidled up next to Rachel's horse, and he climbed from the saddle. "Good boy," he said.

A clap of thunder boomed overhead, and he decided to put the horses in the barn near Rachel's cabin for the night. He quickly led them inside, removed the saddles and gave them some water. He stopped to pet Cleo and check on the pups and noticed Kenny had taken care of them. Affection for the kid mushroomed inside him. In spite of the trauma the little boy had suffered, he still remembered his responsibility.

Swallowing against the pang in his throat, he headed back outside and jogged to Rachel's cabin.

Making certain his gun was safely tucked in the back of his jeans but accessible if he needed it, he rushed up the porch steps and knocked on the door. Rain began to pour, pounding the roof and running off the porch ledge as Rachel opened the door and let him inside.

Her face looked ashen, her hair tangled, her eyes haunted. His gut instinct was to pull her into his arms and assure her everything was all right.

But his conversation with Leon taunted him, and he had to find out the truth once and for all.

"What happened?" Rachel asked.

Johnny removed his Stetson and shook rain from the brim. "It was Burgess. He said your ex offered money to anyone who found you and Kenny."

The color drained from Rachel's face, and she staggered back to the sofa and slumped down on it, then dropped her head into her hands.

Her weary sigh tore at his heart. Her reaction was too honest. There was no way she was lying about how violent her ex-husband was.

Finally, she took a deep breath and looked up at him with a mixture of fear and resignation. "Where is he now?"

Anger simmered inside Johnny, remnants of being used too many times. "I paid him off, Rachel, and warned him that if he came back I'd put a bullet in his head."

Her gasp of shock reverberated in the air, adding to the tension.

"What did you expect me to do?" He strode over, dropped down on his haunches and gripped her arms, forcing her to look at him.

Emotions marred her face. "I…don't know. I… thank you."

Fury rippled through him. "You're thanking me? For what?" he asked in an incredulous voice. "For threatening to kill someone?"

Hating the emotions bombarding him, he released her and paced back and forth, his boots clicking in the tension-laden air. When she didn't answer, he whirled around. "That's not me, Rachel. I'm not a violent man. I know I had some bad press and I got into some brawls when I was on the circuit, but I was drinking and full of myself back then." He pressed his hand over his chest. "I've changed. I don't go around beating up men. I should have called the sheriff and turned the bastard in."

Rachel released a small sob. "I told you I'm sorry. I don't know what else to say. The man tried to kidnap Kenny!"

Johnny strode back to her, and gripped her by

the shoulders. "I know that, and the thought of him hurting that little boy tears me up. But you lied to me, Rachel. You have from the start."

Pain wrenched her expression. "I didn't want to, Johnny, but Rex—"

"Rex what?" His tone was harsh. "Rex hurt you, I guessed that. But I also know there's a warrant out for your arrest. That it says you tried to kill him. For all I know, the man hit you in self-defense."

Rachel leaned back as if he'd physically punched her, a gut-wrenching sound erupting from her throat. "That's not true, Johnny."

"What's not true?" he growled. "That you're not wanted by the law for attempted murder and kidnapping?"

Tears leaked from her big eyes. "Yes, there's a warrant," she whispered in a raw voice. "But the charges are bogus. I did buy a gun to protect myself and my son, but I never shot him. In fact, he tried to strangle me, the last time I saw Rex." Angry now, she turned a wild look on him, then went and retrieved the photo Rex had cut up and shoved it at him. "When Kenny and I got back, Rex left that on Kenny's pillow. What kind of man does that to his son?"

Johnny glanced at the mangled photo and muttered a curse.

"You have no idea what it's like to have someone try to control you. To have him humiliate you and hit you in front of your son."

He started to speak and reached for her, but her eyes dared him to touch her. "To go to bed afraid your husband, the man who vowed to love you, will kill you in the night." She slung her hands out. "I couldn't bear the thought of a man like that raising Kenny. And I have no doubt that one day he will turn his rage on Kenny."

Johnny's stomach roiled. "Rachel—"

"And for your information, I did go to the police. I tried a restraining order. But Rex owns people, Johnny. His father is a judge. He has money and charm and knows how to use it." Disgust tinged her voice. "He tried to make me look unfit. Spread rumors that I was a drunk, that I was the one who hurt Kenny." Her voice cracked, tears spilling over.

Johnny clenched and unclenched his fists. He wanted to kill her ex-husband.

He wanted to hold her and make everything all right.

"Maybe I don't know exactly what you've been through," Johnny said, memories of his own childhood bombarding him. "But I do know exactly what it's like to have your father beat on you. And to have people accuse you of doing something bad that you didn't do."

He also understood what it was like to want to protect her son.

A little boy he was starting to love.

He'd be damned if he'd let Kenny grow up like he had.

For God's sake, when he'd learned Kenny was missing, he'd nearly gone out of his mind with worry. He couldn't imagine the depth of Rachel's fear.

Rachel suddenly ran from the room, and he raced into the bedroom and saw her grab her suitcase again.

Johnny jerked it from her. "You can't keep running. You have to stay."

Rachel's tormented gaze met his. "No," she said, much calmer now. "I've endangered you and everyone else by being selfish. Rex knows where we are now. It's only a matter of time before he attacks me or tries to take Kenny again."

"You're not going anywhere," he said gruffly. "You and Kenny are staying here with me."

"No," Rachel said emphatically. "It's better this way."

"Better for whom?" he bit out. "Not for Kenny. He can't run scared all his life."

She swayed slightly as if he'd knocked the wind from her. "Don't you think I know that? But…I have no choice."

"Yes, you do." He pulled her into his arms and

held her close. "I'll take care of you both, Rachel. Please, just trust me."

She tilted her head back to look into his eyes, and another revelation hit Johnny square in the chest like a bull kicking him hard.

He was in love with Rachel.

No matter what had happened, no matter that she'd lied, he would protect her and Kenny with his life.

RACHEL WANTED TO BELIEVE Johnny more than anything in the world, but reality assailed her. "Johnny, I want to stay, but you don't know Rex like I do. He will buy off the cops, the judges, whoever he needs, to put me away. And the more I think about it, the more certain I am he killed the one judge who went against him."

"You may be right, but I have money, too," Johnny said.

Her heart stuttered, but she shook her head no. "There's no way I'd take your money or ask you to bribe a judge or cop." She placed a loving hand against his cheek. "No way I'd let you ruin your reputation or jeopardize what you and Brody are doing here." Her voice warbled. "The boys, this ranch, they all need you too much."

The doubts she'd seen in his eyes earlier faded. "Trust me," he said. "Let me take care of you and Kenny." He lifted a strand of her hair and brushed it over her shoulder. The gesture was so tender, so sensual that her resistance shattered, her doubts scattering like a tumbleweed blowing in the wind.

Then he cupped her face in his hands and pressed his mouth over hers. Rachel had been alone for so long. Had been frightened and built a protective wall around her heart.

But one touch was all it took for Johnny to make her feel alive and wanted. One look was all it took for her to step off the ledge and fall into his arms

And completely in love with him.

He teased her lips apart with his tongue and delved inside, deepening the kiss and stirring primal needs she could no longer deny. The terror she'd felt earlier when Kenny had gone missing reminded her of how fleeting and precious these moments were, that she had to hold on to her son and savor any happiness that came into her life, no matter how transient.

And Johnny Long was the best thing that had ever happened to her.

She threaded her fingers in his hair and pulled him closer, hungry for more. He seemed to understand and stroked her back, then eased one hand around to cup her breasts. Need flared inside her, and she moaned, silently willing him to make love to her.

He gently pulled back and searched her face.

"Any time you want me to stop, Rachel, all you have to do is say no."

His sensitivity and the gruff, sultry tone to his voice intensified her hunger, and she slid her hands down to unbutton his shirt. One button, two, three, his breath hissed, an erotic sound that ignited her passion.

Then his mouth found hers again, and this time that passion exploded in a rush of tongues mating and hands exploring. Rachel remembered her son, though, and tugged Johnny into her bedroom.

He paused at the door, his breathing labored, and gave her one last opportunity to say no. But she didn't want a way out. Not this time.

She wanted Johnny naked and loving her.

Johnny's heart drummed in his chest, his body hammering home his raging need to be with Rachel. She was vulnerable but strong and so damn beautiful that he felt humbled being invited into her bedroom.

The sound of the door closing as he shut it added an intimacy and aroused him even more. He'd wanted, craved a night in Rachel's bed ever since she'd arrived. The fact that she wanted him after the way she'd been treated intensified his emotions.

Then she gave him a sultry, beckoning look, and he stripped his shirt and tossed it to the floor.

His hat he gently hung on the chair in the corners, then he walked toward her.

When she reached for him and rubbed her fingers across the broad expanse of his chest, his breath became trapped in his lungs. With a teasing smile, she lowered her head and trailed kisses over his torso.

Johnny's body hardened with need, but he allowed her to set the pace. Her kisses were tender but so damn erotic that a second later he thought he'd explode. He eased her back toward the bed, then slowly began to undress her.

Only, Rachel seemed in a hurry. Her breath quickened, her hands flew to help him, and suddenly they were tearing off each other's clothes and falling onto the bed, a tangle of naked limbs and bodies. Their tongues danced and mated again, then he lowered his head to take one firm ripe nipple into his mouth and suckle her. He raked his other hand down her abdomen and found the soft nest of curls at the juncture of her thighs. She was wet and he slipped one finger inside her.

She writhed beneath him, urging him on, and he spread her legs and dipped his tongue into her honeyed sweetness. Her moan of pleasure sent a million sensations pummeling him, and when she cried out his name and her body convulsed with pleasure, he rose above her, grabbed a condom from his jeans pocket, rolled it on and teased her legs apart with his sex.

Her hand came down to grip him, making his erection throb, but he let her guide him inside her. Her warm, wet body enveloped him, her muscles clinched his thickness, and he plunged deeper, then withdrew, then filled her again. She wrapped her legs around him and he set a rhythm, rocking inside her, stroking, filling, taking, giving.

And when she clutched his hips and lifted her own, coaxing him to move deeper, then whispered that she was coming, his own release spiraled out of control and he lost himself inside her.

Chapter Nineteen

Rachel rolled over and curled in Johnny's arms, sated and happier than she'd ever been with a man. She buried her head against his shoulder, and he pulled her closer against him and kissed her again. She savored the moment as they lay entwined, hearts beating, breath slowly steadying, erotic sensations tingling through her body.

Exhaustion pulled at her, but she didn't want to go to sleep. She wanted to languish in the pleasure he had given her.

Johnny had reminded her that lovemaking was supposed to be about love.

And she was totally in love with Johnny.

But Johnny was a star, a man who was only donating time here at the ranch, a man who had his own life to go back to. Not a man who wanted or deserved to be saddled with a ready-made family with trouble on their tails.

Johnny nuzzled her neck, then stroked her arm gently with his fingers, and she closed her eyes, relaxing in his embrace. Outside, the rain slowed to a drizzle, the pattering on the roof a soft hypnotic rhythm, cocooning them into their own private world.

"I like the rain," Johnny said.

"Why?" Rachel whispered.

"Because it brings new life to the ranch," Johnny murmured.

Rachel realized he was right. The rain would make the grass grow and water the flowers and bring spring into full bloom.

Just like Johnny had done with her heart.

She kissed him tenderly, then he deepened the kiss and moments later they made love again. Slowly, tenderly, languidly, tasting and exploring…

And for the first time in two years, Rachel forgot that she was a wanted woman and allowed herself to dream that she and Kenny and Johnny could be a family.

A sense of peace washed over her as another orgasm rocked through her in perfect timing with Johnny's.

Then he held her again, and she finally fell into a deep sleep. A sleep filled with dreams of marriage and babies and a life that she hadn't dared dream about for the past two years.

JOHNNY WOKE AT THE CRACK of dawn. He rolled sideways to make sure Rachel was still in his arms, that last night hadn't been a figment of his imagination.

His chest heaved with relief when he saw she was still there.

Then his body stirred once more. Early morning sunlight seeped through the sheers and painted glowing lines across her beautiful face. God... He could get used to waking up beside her every day.

The tip of one naked breast glowed in the sunlight, and he ached to kiss it and make love to her again. But reality seeped in. It was morning, and Rachel's son was sleeping in the next room and might wake up any minute.

He didn't want Kenny to find him in Rachel's bed.

Not until they were ma— What the hell was he thinking?

Johnny Long was a bachelor. Not husband or father material.

Besides, they still had to deal with her ex and the charges against her.

His phone buzzed, and he checked the number. Brody.

Damn. He'd promised he'd explain the situation this morning and he'd better get his butt over and do just that.

Rachel sighed as he kissed her cheek, then he tucked the covers over her and rose. He hurriedly dressed, then grabbed his hat and tiptoed out the door, closing it gently so as not to wake her. The ground was still damp from the night's rain, but the sun glinted off the water droplets clinging to the grass, making them shimmer like diamonds.

He texted Brody that he'd be there in half an hour, then retrieved the horses he and Rachel had ridden the night before, mounted Soldier and led her horse back to the stables. One of the ranch hands was already mucking stalls and he asked him to take care of the animals.

Then he rushed to the main house, took a quick shower, poured himself a cup of coffee in the kitchen and went to meet Brody.

"All right," Brody said, "what's going on, Johnny?"

Johnny cleared his throat, then spilled the whole story.

"Dammit, Johnny, why didn't you tell me this sooner?" Brody asked.

"Because at first it was just suspicion."

Brody leaned back in his desk chair. "We have to talk to the sheriff."

"No." Johnny's emphatic tone brought an eye raise from his friend.

"Why not? If this Rex guy is as dangerous as you say, we can't let it go. In fact, you should have turned Burgess in last night."

Johnny swallowed hard. "Maybe, but I believe

Rachel, Brody. You and I both know money can buy people. And God knows, the press can add its own spin. Look how they crucified me."

Brody drummed his fingers on the desk. "So, what now?"

"You hired extra security. Let's alert them to watch out for Rachel's ex and for Burgess. And I'll personally guard Rachel and Kenny."

Brody studied him for a long, tension-filled moment. "This is not like you, Johnny. What's going on between you and this woman?"

Johnny hesitated, a lie on the tip of his tongue. But lies had landed him in trouble when he was younger. And he respected Brody and what he was doing too much not to be honest.

"I care about her and the boy," Johnny said. "Besides, we've worked too hard on the rodeo and setting up this ranch. If this story goes public, it could cost us big time."

"Which would make Copeland damn happy." Brody chewed the inside of his cheek. "All right, we'll play it your way for now. But if Rachel's ex shows up and causes trouble, I won't hesitate to call the sheriff. Rachel will have to deal with the fallout."

Johnny nodded. Brody was right. But Rachel would not have to deal with the fallout alone. He would do whatever he could to help her.

Kenny's terrified face the night before flashed

in his mind. In fact, he would like to meet her ex face to face, himself.

And when he did, Johnny would convince him to leave Rachel alone. If he didn't, the lowlife would be sorry.

RACHEL FELT THE EMPTY bed and immediately missed Johnny. She rolled to her side and clutched the pillow Johnny had slept on, inhaling his rugged masculine odor and letting it wipe away the scent of Rex's cologne.

She had no idea where she and Johnny would go from here, but she knew what she wanted.

Only what she wanted was impossible.

She checked the clock. Kenny would be up soon, so she jumped in the shower and quickly shampooed and rinsed her hair, almost hating to wash the scent of Johnny off her.

But she had to get ready for the day.

She'd barely dressed when footsteps pattered across the floor and Kenny appeared in her doorway.

"Mom, is the bad man coming back?"

"No, honey. We're safe now." Rachel rushed to him and hugged him, although, even as she reassured him he was safe, fear crowded her chest. Burgess might be gone, but Rex would hire another.

Or come himself.

It was only a matter of time. She'd been deluding herself into thinking otherwise.

But she couldn't leave until after the rodeo. She couldn't deprive Kenny of this one memory, not when he'd dreamed about it forever.

Kenny hurried to check on Cleo and the pups. She let him play with them for a few minutes, then Cleo followed the two of them to the dining hall. When Blair entered, her eyes looked puffy, her expression contrite. Rachel knew the poor girl blamed herself for Kenny's disappearance, so she pulled her aside. "I need to talk to you in private."

A sliver of apprehension streaked the girl's face, then Rachel explained that her ex had been following her and Kenny.

"It's not your fault, Blair. He hired this man to kidnap Kenny." Rachel fought a shudder. "I have custody, but Kenny's father is violent. I should have told you before, but I didn't think he'd find us here. But he did. So please keep an extra careful eye on Kenny."

"I promise I won't let him out of my sight." The young woman squeezed Rachel's hand.

"Thanks." Rachel went to explain the circumstances to Ms. Ellen. With everyone on alert and the extra security Brody had hired, hopefully Rex would be dissuaded and leave them alone.

But that was a pipe dream, and she kept her eyes peeled for him to show any minute.

THE NEXT THREE DAYS, Johnny kept an eye on Rachel and Kenny, but he didn't allow himself to sleep with her again.

Not that he didn't want to. Just the memory of her naked in his arms stirred his hunger. But sleeping with her was a distraction, and he had to remain alert. Letting his guard down was too dangerous.

Besides, there were a thousand details to handle in preparation for the rodeo. The kids were excited, the vendors had set up booths, the ads had been placed, the TV interview had aired and all the investors had arrived to help make certain the safety specifications for the rodeo events were up to par.

Each of the investors had offered to man events and participate in a grand-finale exhibition that would hopefully help draw a larger crowd. Johnny was on the billing as the grand finale, but he wanted to downplay his role. Still, the idea of showing off in front of Rachel gave him a small thrill.

Excitement hummed in the air the night of the rodeo. Johnny and the other ranchers rechecked the venues, stables, chutes and animals to verify everything was in order and up to safety regulations. Counselors worked alongside the boys to set up the pony rides, face branding, horseshoes, a lasso contest and other events for the smaller children. His sister and Lucy offered to handle the face-branding booth, and Lucy was the first customer and chose a bright red ladybug to match her hair.

Johnny wondered if Kim would avoid Brandon again, and had been surprised that she'd stayed for the rodeo. After he broke her heart five years ago and married another woman, she had always made sure she wasn't around when he and Brandon had gotten together. Then again, Lucy's excited pleas were impossible to resist. She reminded him of Kim as a little girl. Lucy followed Kenny around as Kim had followed him and Brandon and Carter.

"Family picture!" Lucy said as the cameraman shot candids of the preparations. Kim hesitated, but took Lucy's hand and the three of them posed for the camera.

Volunteers had signed up to man ticket booths, and Johnny was impressed with the lines forming. Families, teenagers and kids chattered excitedly, hurrying to participate in the pre-rodeo activities and buy refreshments and souvenirs. Others perused the silent auction and bought raffle tickets for the items Johnny had solicited from various friends and sponsors in the rodeo circuit.

He went to check on Rachel before the show began and found her and Kenny in the barn with Cleo and the pups. "I had to feed them before the rodeo," Kenny said.

The puppies had started waddling around now and were licking Kenny's hands. Cleo lay at his feet as if she worshipped the boy. Johnny wanted Kenny to have at least one of the dogs, but he'd have to talk to Rachel first.

Kenny giggled as one of the puppies tried to crawl up his chest, and Johnny laughed. "If you want to participate in the games before the rodeo starts, it's time."

Kenny hugged the puppy, then gently set him on the ground. "I have to go, little one. I'll see you later."

Rachel looked nervous but excited. Johnny's nerves felt raw. Security had been easy to maintain during a normal day, but with the crowd tonight, Rex might be able to sneak in.

He had to stay on his toes.

Together, the three of them walked over to the arena for the children's games. Johnny and Rachel joined Kim, then they watched Kenny and Lucy enjoy the games. Lucy won the stick-pony ride, laughing as she twirled around at the finish and bowed. Johnny glanced up and saw Brandon in the distance, helping some boys line up the barrels, and felt a pang of sadness over the rift between Kim and Brandon, and the three of them and Carter.

"Kenny has quite an arm," Johnny said as the little boy tossed the horseshoes.

A wistful look passed across Rachel's face. "I've never seen him so happy."

Johnny heard the longing in her voice and wondered if she was considering leaving after the show. His heart tugged painfully at the thought.

He wanted to ask them to stay. Or maybe to go with him to his ranch.

But he held his tongue. They still had to deal with Rex before he could even contemplate a future with Rachel.

The next half hour, Kenny and Lucy participated in the three-legged race, wheelbarrow races, cactus hat throw and rope-tying contest. After every event, Kenny looked up at them, then tipped his Stetson, a big grin on his face.

Finally, it was time for the main rodeo events to begin. Kim rushed with Lucy to find a seat. Rachel caught Johnny's arm as her son hurried to join the other competitors. "Johnny, you'll make sure he's safe?"

"I promise." Johnny squeezed her hand. "If you see your ex or anyone suspicious, buzz me or let security know immediately."

She nodded and claimed a seat beside Kim and Lucy as the announcer welcomed the spectators, introduced the sponsors and began announcing the events. "Now let's give a round of applause for our barrel racers."

Johnny met the boys in the stable, his gaze

scanning the crowd. The past two days had been the lull before the storm.

Johnny had a bad feeling Rex would strike tonight.

RACHEL TRIED TO RELAX and enjoy the show, but she constantly scanned the crowd and the property for Rex.

Applause broke out, drawing her attention back to the arena, then the announcer called the first contestant's name. Three kids ran the barrel races before Kenny, and she held her breath as she watched him maneuver his horse around the barrels. Dust spewed from the horse's hooves. Kenny's hat flew off as he swung around the third barrel and drove the horse around the last one, then circled back.

Rachel stood, clapping her heart out. "Way to go, Kenny!"

Kim and Lucy clapped, cheering his name, too.

When Kenny finished, he spun the horse around and waved to her, his face beaming.

"Now, for our winners," the announcer said.

The boys lined up on horseback to receive their ribbons, and tears of joy pricked Rachel's eyes. "Kenny Simmons takes third place, Bobby Martin second and Willie Sutter is our first-place winner!" Kenny didn't seem to care that he hadn't won, and rode over and hugged Willie, the two of them locking arms as cameras snapped their pictures.

Next came calf roping, which Ricardo won. His look of pride as he accepted the ribbon touched Rachel's heart. The competition continued, with each of the campers participating in at least one event, and all of them laughing and shouting with excitement as they cheered each other on.

Trick riding came next, featuring some of the older boys and Brandon, Johnny's friend who brought the crowd to a standing ovation with his showy style. She couldn't help but notice Kim watching him with a bittersweet look and wondered if there had been something between the two of them once.

An intermission followed, and the boys entered a reserved section of the stand to watch the grand finale—the investors performing for the kids. Rachel leaned forward, her heart drumming as the announcer introduced the ranchers—Brody Bloodworth, Johnny Long, Brandon Woodstock, Miles McGregor and Mason Blackpaw.

"Johnny looks great today," Kim said. "He's most at home in the saddle."

Rachel nodded, her heart fluttering at the sight of his handsome face.

"He cares about you and Kenny," Kim said softly.

Rachel blushed. "He's been great for Kenny."

"It's not just Kenny," Kim said. "I've never seen him look at a woman the way he looks at you."

She did not want to have this conversation. "Kim—"

"Johnny got a bad rap as a playboy in the media," Kim continued, cutting her off. "But he's a really good guy. I don't know if he told you about our parents, but our mama took off one day and our daddy used to beat Johnny."

Rachel sighed, hurting for Johnny and admiring him for taking care of his sister. No wonder he had sensed the truth about her situation.

"He took care of me growing up," Kim continued, "and then…when Lucy came along. I don't know what I would have done without him."

Emotions swirled in Rachel's throat. "I know how difficult it is to be a single mother."

Kim's gaze met hers, her eyes filled with questions, although she didn't ask them. Instead, she lowered her voice. "Just don't hurt him. He acts tough, but he's really a teddy bear at heart."

Rachel clenched her hands in her lap. "I…know."

"Let's welcome our exhibition riders!" the announcer shouted, bringing the crowd to their feet. "First we have our bareback and trick riders."

Kim's words taunted Rachel as she watched the show. Maybe she should leave tonight after the rodeo, make a clean break. Save her and Johnny both more heartbreak before she fell even deeper for the man.

Next came a roping show by Brandon and Mason who demonstrated techniques for breaking a wild horse. Then they had a small break before the highlight—Johnny riding a bull.

Kenny and two other boys darted toward the concession stand, and she started to follow but spotted a security guard nearby and sighed in relief. When the intermission ended, Kenny and Willie moved up to the fence to watch Johnny.

"We are honored tonight to have our very own rodeo celebrity with us!" The announcer introduced Johnny, citing his accomplishments and awards on the rodeo circuit. Everyone burst into applause, shouting his name in chorus. "Johnny, Johnny, Johnny!"

Rachel's chest ached as she watched Johnny climb onto the bull in the chute and wave to the crowd. People jumped to their feet, clapping and roaring his name again.

The bull was bucking and growling inside the chute, waiting to be let out.

The beast could crush a man with his weight, if it didn't gore Johnny with his horns first. The memory of Johnny saving Kenny from one still haunted her.

She glanced at Kenny again, and saw him leaning against the fence in total awe. The announcer hushed the crowd, anticipation rippling through the stands, then seconds later Johnny climbed onto the bull. He gripped the reins tightly with one hand, threw his left hand up in the air, the chute opened, and the bull raced out, bucking and dropping his head forward, digging his paws in, doing his best to throw Johnny off.

The clock ticked the seconds away, the crowd collectively holding their breaths. Rachel's heart banged against her chest as each second crawled by. She couldn't stand it if Johnny got hurt.

Then out of the corner of her eye, she saw someone grab Kenny's arm. Then he angled his face to look at her and he sent her a sinister grin.

Rex.

Panic slammed into her, and she jumped up. "Kenny!" She spun toward Kim. "Get Brody and security!"

Kenny tried to pull away, but Rex hauled him up against him and dashed into the barn.

Rachel screamed and vaulted down the bleacher steps after them.

Chapter Twenty

The roar of the crowd spurred Johnny to hold on tighter as the bull bucked and spun around trying to pitch him off. He ate dust, his Stetson flew off and his neck jerked with the force of the bull's anger.

Cheers turned into chants as the fans yelled his name. He hugged his legs tighter around the beast's body, bouncing hard as he glanced at the clock. A couple more seconds and he'd beat his own record.

The crowd began to count with the timer, the announcer urging them on. He glanced toward Kenny but didn't see him. Then he caught a glimpse of Rachel racing from the stands and knew something was wrong.

Forgetting about the crowd and the countdown, he released his hold on the bull and let it throw him. He'd been tossed enough times to know how to fall and he rolled on the ground away from the animal. The pen gate flew open and Brandon and

Brody raced in, driving the bull toward the chute while he jumped the fence.

Oblivious to his panic, the crowd clapped and sang his name again, but Johnny didn't care about the accolades. He was too worried about Rachel and Kenny.

Sweat beaded on his skin as he jogged through the stable to the back exit searching for them. Rachel was running toward the parking area. A second later, he spotted a dark-haired man dragging Kenny into a black town car.

Dammit.

He felt for his weapon, but realized he didn't have it, then glanced around for security, but security was busy covering the arena.

"Stop, Rex!" Rachel shouted. "Don't do this!"

Kenny was kicking and screaming, trying to break free. Johnny raced down the hill toward the car, but Rachel was closer.

"Please, Rex, it's me you want, not him!" Rachel cried.

The man hurled Kenny against the door edge. "He's my son," Rex shouted. "I warned you not to leave me."

Rachel lunged toward him. "He's just a little boy, and you're scaring him."

"You're right," Rex snarled. With an evil leer, he shoved Kenny to the ground and grabbed Rachel. Kenny yelped as he hit the dirt.

Fury filled Johnny.

"Run, Kenny!" Rachel shouted. "Run!"

Johnny had almost caught up with them, but Rex yanked Rachel against the car, pulled a gun and pressed it against Rachel's temple.

Johnny froze, paralyzed with fear. "Let the boy go," Johnny said, afraid if he moved the man would kill Rachel.

"He's my son," Rex growled. "Not yours."

"That's right, and he loves his mother," Johnny said quietly. "You don't want to hurt him by hurting her, do you?"

Kenny crawled to his knees and looked up at his father, terror streaking his little face. "Please, Daddy, let Mommy go!"

Rex's eyes shot daggers at Kenny. "Shut up, kid."

"It's okay, Kenny." Johnny pulled the terrified little boy behind him to protect him. "Do the right thing, Presley."

"She's my wife," Rex growled. "We said vows. She's not leaving me."

"She already did," Johnny said. "You have to accept it."

"No, I don't." Rex sneered and tightened his grip around Rachel's neck.

"Rex, please," Rachel begged. "Let me go for Kenny's sake."

The SOB used his tongue to swipe her cheek, and Johnny saw red.

"No way, baby. You're mine. Let your lover boy call the police," Rex said with a sarcastic laugh. "While you're at it, Mr. Rodeo Boy, tell them I'm bringing in a wanted felon."

So Rachel hadn't lied about how evil her ex was or that he had cops in his pocket.

Pent-up rage boiled inside Johnny, and he inched forward, knowing a sudden move would set the bastard off.

Rex waved the gun in front of Rachel again. "Get back or I'll kill her right here."

"Daddy, no!" Kenny wrestled free from Johnny and lunged at his father, beating him with his fists. "Let Mommy go!"

Rex cursed, then shoved Kenny to the ground so hard that he fell backward.

Johnny grabbed Kenny and hauled the poor kid up, hating Rex with every fiber of his being.

Rachel gave Johnny a beseeching look. "Please take care of Kenny."

Rex yanked Rachel by the hair and shoved her into the front seat of his car, then pushed her over to the passenger side and climbed in. Kenny screamed and tried to run toward the car, but Johnny caught him. Then Rex aimed at Johnny's feet and fired a shot.

Johnny jumped back to dodge the bullet, protecting Kenny with his body, then Rex started the engine and raced away.

Johnny spun around, hunting for security and saw Brody jogging toward him. The rodeo was ending, the crowd beginning to spill out. A minute later and traffic would be clogged.

"What's going on?" Brody yelled.

"Rachel's ex has her!" Johnny handed Kenny to Brody. "Take care of him, Brody. I have to go after her."

Kenny tried to wiggle free again. "I'm going, too. She's my mommy. I gots to save her."

"No," Johnny said, tempering his anger. "It's too dangerous, buddy. Just trust me and go with Brody."

Tears ran down Kenny's face. "But Mommy…"

"You are a big man, a brave guy, a real cowboy, Kenny." Johnny squeezed Kenny's arm. "But let me finish this. I'll bring your mommy back to you, son. I promise. Now hurry, go with Brody so I can catch up with them."

Kenny's chin quivered, but he nodded, then Brody tossed him his keys. "Take my SUV. It's parked by the fence."

Johnny caught the keys, then broke into a dead run. He jumped in the SUV, started the engine and punched the accelerator. The SUV bounced over the pasture, then onto the narrow road leading to the highway. He spotted the town car ahead rounding a curve, and stomped on the gas, then chased it onto the main road.

The town car sped up, tires screeching as Rex took another curve going too fast, then Johnny saw Rachel fighting him for the steering wheel. The car careened sideways, hit a pothole, swerved the opposite way and skated along the embankment. Dirt and gravel spewed from the vehicle, tires squealing again as Rex struggled to keep it on the road.

Johnny was closing in, but Rex raised his gun and slammed the butt of it down against Rachel's head. She fell sideways, then collapsed.

Cold rage unlike anything Johnny had ever felt heated his blood, and he accelerated and slammed into the town car's bumper. The sedan skidded sideways, and Rex swerved onto a dirt road. Johnny careened after him, spitting dust as he banged into the man's bumper again.

The road wound back and forth for a mile, then Rex swung the car around and headed straight toward him. Johnny thought he was going to hit him, but Rex screeched to a stop, jumped out and fired at him. Glass shattered and sprayed the ground, and Johnny jerked sideways as another bullet pelted the door.

Johnny hit the brakes, screeched to a stop, landing sideways, his front bumper only a few feet from the town car's. Using every ounce of control he possessed, Johnny counted the bullets as Rex unloaded two more at him. Cursing, he opened his door and crouched behind it, using it as a shield.

Rachel still hadn't moved. Johnny's chest clenched with fear. Every second counted.

Rage fueled his adrenaline, and he inched back behind his car, ducking low and circling behind Rex's car to launch a surprise attack.

He almost made it, too, but his foot hit a twig. It snapped and Rex jerked his head around. Johnny threw himself forward and grabbed Rex by the shoulders, forcing him to drop the gun. They rolled and fought, Johnny's temper escalating as he punched the man repeatedly.

Then a groan from the seat echoed toward him, and for just a second he eased up. That moment gave Rex the chance he needed, and he crawled for the gun. Johnny tried to reach it first, but Rex snagged it, whipped it around and fired.

Pain rocked through Johnny's chest as the bullet ripped into him. He staggered back at the impact, falling into the dirt, and Rex jumped on top of him, then raised the pistol at his head.

Johnny's life flashed in front of him. His mistakes. His cocky attitude, an attitude he'd adopted to cover up the loneliness of not having a family to love. A family who loved him back.

Dammit. He wanted that family and he wanted it with Rachel.

But he might lose her now, and he'd never even told her that he loved her.

RACHEL SLOWLY ROUSED from unconsciousness, her head throbbing. She lifted her hand to wipe away the blood trickling down her forehead, momentarily disoriented. But flashes of Rex dragging Kenny toward his car rippled back, and she remembered trading herself for her son.

Squinting against the darkness, she pulled herself up, scrambling to see where Rex had taken her. Probably some isolated place where he could kill her and dump her body.

Where was he?

Blinking to clear her head, she crawled to the driver's side hoping to find the keys but heard a moan of pain from outside and suddenly spotted Rex. Her lungs tightened.

Rex had Johnny pinned down, and was waving his gun above Johnny's face.

"You're gonna die for messing with my woman," Rex growled.

Johnny moaned, and Rachel realized he'd been shot. "You won't get away."

Anger churned through Rachel. Johnny had been so good to her and Kenny. He'd saved their lives.

She couldn't let her ex-husband kill him.

Adrenaline fueled her, and she threw herself on

top of Rex. Her surprise attack sent the gun flying across the ground. She pummeled Rex with her fists, beating his head until he rolled off Johnny. Blood soaked Johnny's shirt, and a sob caught in her throat. Rex threw her off him with such force that her head connected with the ground, knocking the wind from her.

Then Rex bellowed and lunged for her.

Rachel had been beaten by him one too many times. She dodged his blow, then rolled sideways, pushed to her hands and knees and crawled toward the gun. Rex clawed at her ankle, and she shoved her other foot back and kicked him in the face with the heel of her boot. He yelped in pain and anger, then scrambled for her, but she scurried toward the weapon, digging in the dirt as she went. Rex slapped his hand on the back of her calf and dragged her backward. She clawed for something to fight him with, kicking wildly, then her fingers closed around a stick.

She swung it back, stabbing at his face, earning another cry of pain as she jabbed his eye.

"You bitch!" Cursing like a sailor, he dove for her again, but Rachel dived for the gun. She grabbed it, rolled to her side and aimed just as he jumped her.

The gun went off, the sound bouncing off the night air, then Rex grunted and his body slumped forward on top of her. Rachel collapsed, pushing at him, desperate to get him off her.

A wet stickiness soaked her, and then Rex's eyes went wide and glassy. Nausea clogged her throat.

She had killed him.

A hysterical scream tore from her, but through the haze of her panic, she remembered Johnny was hurt. Trembling all over, she tossed the gun into the dirt and tried to stand. Her legs wobbled as she ran toward Johnny.

Please don't be dead...

Fear clawed at her chest as she dropped down to see if he was breathing. Her own breaths were coming in noisy pants, her hands shaking as she placed one of them on his heart. Then his eyes slipped open and she felt the slow rise and fall of his chest.

"Rachel," he whispered.

"Shh," she said softly. "It's over. Rex is dead, Johnny."

Only it wasn't over. Not for her.

She stumbled to the car and found Rex's cell phone. She had to get help for Johnny.

But then the sheriff would take her away. And after all she'd been through, she'd lose Kenny.

But she loved Johnny too much to let him die, so she punched the sheriff's number.

JOHNNY FADED IN AND OUT of consciousness, his mind blurred by pain and drugs as the paramedics arrived and began an IV. Blue lights from the ambulance and police swirled against the darkness, then Brody was talking to him, telling him Rex was dead, and the sheriff appeared, asking him questions.

What happened? Who shot first? Rachel killed her husband? What did he know about her past? Was he aware there was a warrant out for her arrest? Had she kidnapped her son?

Johnny searched for Rachel, but it was hard to see anything from the gurney. He vaguely remembered telling her Brody had Kenny, then her holding his head in her hands, stroking his forehead and murmuring soft words to him while they'd waited for the ambulance. But then the sheriff arrived and he'd passed out...

The medics lifted him into the ambulance and he raised his head and finally saw her. His heart wrenched.

The sheriff was handcuffing her and putting her into the back of his car.

Johnny breathed through his teeth. "No...can't arrest her...Kenny."

But his words died as the painkillers took over and he slipped into unconsciousness.

RACHEL FOUGHT A SOB as the sheriff locked her inside his squad car, flipped on the siren and careened down the dirt road. The coroner was taking care of Rex. Johnny was headed to the hospital. And Kenny was safe at the ranch with Brody and Ms. Ellen.

But she was on her way to jail.

Lights swirled in the night, the echo of the siren blasting, a reminder that there was nowhere to run. Not anymore.

Tears leaked from her eyes, and she doubled over, nausea gripping her. She loved Johnny, but he had been shot trying to protect her.

Kim's warning taunted her. She hadn't meant to get Johnny hurt, but he'd nearly died because of her.

Johnny was better off without her in his life.

But God help her, she wasn't sorry Rex was dead. At least he couldn't turn his wrath on her son.

Only, who would take care of Kenny now?

Chapter Twenty-One

Johnny railed against the doctors' orders to stay in bed after the surgery. He cursed the injustice of seeing Rachel hauled away in handcuffs.

And he nearly broke down and cried when Brody told him Kenny had been taken to a foster home.

By God, he was not going to stay in this damn hospital another second. He was going to the courthouse for Rachel's hearing and convince the judge that she had been a victim.

"Listen, Johnny," Brody said. "An attorney is working on her release."

"I'll pay whatever it costs," Johnny said. "And if we have to bring criminal charges against the cops that bastard had on his payroll, we'll do it."

Johnny ripped the IV from his arm, then reached for the clothes Brody had brought him.

"You can't leave now," Brody said. "The doctor hasn't released you yet."

"Either drive me to the courthouse or step

aside," Johnny said. "Rachel is not going to spend another night in jail."

For God's sake, she'd already been there two nights. No telling what had happened to her. And poor Kenny… Foster homes sometimes held horrors of their own.

Brody relented and made a phone call while Johnny yanked on his clothes. His chest hurt like the devil, but the pain from the bullet that had lodged within an inch of his heart didn't compare to the agony of thinking that he might lose Rachel and Kenny.

When Brody returned, his expression was grave, but he helped Johnny down the hall and into the elevator. A half hour later, Johnny clutched his chest, battling for each breath as he and Brody strode into the courtroom.

Rachel's pale face tore at him as a guard led her in in handcuffs. Her gaze met his, and anguish and despair darkened her eyes. He tried to silently telegraph to her that everything would be okay.

But was it going to be? What if the judge didn't listen and she went to jail?

The judge called the hearing to order and the next few minutes passed, filled with legal jargon and formalities. Then the door opened and Brandon and Ms. Ellen and the other boys, counselors and ranch hands filed in. Johnny's throat clogged with emotions as he realized they were there to support him and Rachel. The BBL had become a big family. Even Ricardo, who had first put the snake on Rachel's bed, looked incensed and protective as the charges against Rachel were read.

Then Rachel's lawyer called Johnny to the stand. He was sworn in, then relayed exactly what had happened the night he'd been shot.

"Rex Presley tried to kidnap his son, then took Rachel at gunpoint, assaulted her in his vehicle, then opened fire on me."

Rachel's handcuffed hands were clenched on top of the table, tears brimming in her eyes as she stared at him. He wanted to go to her and hold her and assure her that he loved her so badly that he could hardly talk.

After he testified, the judge surprised him by calling Kenny to the stand.

Kenny looked small and scared, but then glanced at Johnny and squared his little shoulders as if he was a big man, and Johnny remembered telling him that a real cowboy lived by a code of ethics and told the truth.

Kenny swallowed hard, then looked at his mother and began to talk.

"My daddy…I loved him," Kenny said in a quiet voice. "But he wasn't a very nice man."

The room seemed to still, the silence ominous as Kenny gave a detailed account of the way his father had treated his mother, everything from calling her cruel, ugly names to hitting her to threatening them both.

By the time he was finished, there wasn't a dry eye in the courtroom, including the men's. Rachel's heart was on her face as she struggled to control her emotions. But shame also reddened her cheeks.

Johnny gritted his teeth. Hadn't he felt that same shame when his father had hit him? Shame he hadn't deserved any more than Rachel or Kenny did?

He hoped Rex Presley was rotting in his grave.

Johnny vowed to spend the rest of his life convincing both of them that they were lovable and hadn't been to blame.

THE JUDGE POUNDED HIS GAVEL. "Ms. Presley, in light of the evidence and testimony I've heard today, and evidence pointing to Rex Presley as the prime suspect in the murder of a prominent judge and his wife, I'm dismissing all charges against you. You are free to go."

Shock echoed through Rachel's body as the courtroom erupted into cheers and the officer removed Rachel's handcuffs. Kenny raced to her and she swept him up in her arms, tears flowing. She and her son were free now. Free to have a real life. Kenny clung to her, his chest heaving.

"You did great, bud. But I'm sorry you had to talk in court."

Kenny pulled back and looked up at her, his arms still looped around her neck. "I just tolded the truth, Mommy. That's what cowboys do."

She laughed through her tears and hugged him again, then Ms. Ellen was hugging her, and Johnny approached. His tanned skin looked pale, his arm was in a sling and pain was etched in his eyes, but he was also smiling.

"You don't have to run anymore, Rachel."

She knew he had footed the bill for her lawyer. "I…thank you, Johnny. I don't know how to repay you."

He shook his head and started to say something else, but the kids gathered around, cutting him off. They were clapping Kenny on the back and treating him like a hero. She couldn't believe they had all shown up to support her.

She'd been alone so long that she didn't know how to handle the instant closeness she felt with them.

She didn't want to let any of them go.

Although, because she'd lied to Brody and had endangered others, Brody might insist she leave.

And even if he allowed her and Kenny to stay at the ranch, Johnny would be leaving to go home. She sighed.

He would take her heart with him when he did.

JOHNNY WANTED TO GRAB Rachel and Kenny up in a hug, but everyone had swarmed around them and, dammit, he was feeling light-headed.

He hated to be weak, but this bullet had knocked him on his butt.

"You need to go back to the hospital," Brody said.

"No way, take me back to the ranch." He stepped forward but had to grip the rail to keep from passing out. "About Rachel—"

"Ms. Ellen offered to drive her back to the ranch."

Johnny wanted to protest, but the room swayed and he was so damn weak that he staggered sideways like a drunk. So he let Brody lead him outside and cart him back to the ranch. Twenty-four hours later, he stirred from a dead sleep, sore and achy and disoriented. He hadn't talked to Rachel since the hearing.

What if she had taken Kenny and they'd already left? He had to talk to her, tell her that he loved her.

But what if she didn't love him in return?

He dragged himself from bed and stared at himself in the mirror. Thick beard stubble and gritty eyes made him look like a hellion. He ran some water in the sink, lathered his face and shaved, then climbed in the shower. A half hour later, he was dressed and feeling somewhat human again.

He was even hungry for the first time since the shooting, so he went down to the kitchen, grabbed some coffee and a piece of toast, then yanked on his Stetson and headed outside.

Night was setting in, moonlight glimmering off the path to Rachel's cabin. The ranch seemed eerily quiet after the excitement of the rodeo, and the first camp session was drawing to a close. In the distance, he spotted a campfire and realized the counselors were holding the closing ceremonies tonight.

If Rachel and Kenny hadn't left, they would be there.

He strode toward the site, voices and laughter reaching him in the evening breeze. In the distance, he heard the sound of cows mooing and horses galloping, sounds that meant home.

He paused at the edge of the camp, searching for Rachel and her son. When he found them across the way, he breathed in relief.

The counselors were announcing the final awards.

"Ricardo earns the award for the most points scored in the individual events, and Willie receives an award for the best sport."

Blair took the podium with a wide grin. "And our last award goes to Kenny Presley for honesty and bravery."

Rachel's face lit with pride as Kenny stepped

up and accepted the award. Everyone clapped and cheered, then the counselors started a round of songs. Rachel glanced at him across the campfire, and their gazes locked.

She looked so damn beautiful that his heart stopped.

He swallowed back emotions, then walked toward her. She met him outside the campfire beneath a Texas red oak.

"Johnny…" Pain laced her voice. "I was so worried about you."

"And I was afraid you'd be gone."

"Brody said I could stay and work here."

A moment of insecurity clawed at Johnny. What if he confessed his love and she couldn't return it? What if she'd only needed him because of her ex? "Do you want to stay?"

Her eyes glowed in the moonlight, crystal pools of longing and need and vulnerability, all the things that had attracted him to her in the first place.

But something else sparked there, as well. Something that gave him courage.

"Kenny and I do love it here," she said softly. "And Kenny adores Cleo and the pups and riding and…everything about ranch life."

"What about you?"

Rachel glanced down at her hands where she'd

knotted them together. "I love it, too. I feel like we've finally found a family. A home."

Was it just the ranch she loved, or did she love him?

"I want you and Kenny to be happy," he said in a gruff voice. Hell, he was messing this up. "But I have to go back to my own spread for a while."

Rachel nodded, then looked up at him and his heart melted. "I understand, Johnny. You have your own life. I'll pay you back for the lawyer fees."

"I don't want your money, Rachel." Johnny had been a cocky show-off once, had women throwing themselves at him. But insecurity struck him now. Rachel wasn't a rodeo groupie. She was special and this was real love. What if she crushed his heart?

Go for it, man. You can't let her walk away. You can't lose her.

His palms were sweating as he cleared his throat. "Rachel, I…I'd like for you and Kenny to go with me."

There, he'd said it. Put his heart on the line.

Rachel's eyes narrowed slightly. "You want me to cook at your ranch?"

He hesitated. "Well, if you want to cook, that's fine. But I already have a cook for the ranch hands."

"I don't understand." She sucked in a sharp

breath. "Are you offering me a job, Johnny?" This time hurt and a note of anger tinged her voice.

Johnny gulped. Hell, no, not a job. "I...that's not exactly what I meant." He took a step closer, summoned his courage and dropped to one knee. "I love you, Rachel. I want to marry you and be a father to Kenny."

The flash of anger he'd seen in her eyes turned to shock and then joy. "You want to marry me?"

He nodded, then gripped her hand in his and kissed her palm. "You mean everything to me, Rachel. I want us to make a life together, and I want to be a father to Kenny, and he can bring one of the pups with him and have his own horse at my place, and we'll come back here and volunteer—"

Rachel squealed with delight, then dropped to her knees and threw her arms around him. "I love you, too, Johnny."

"Then you'll marry me?"

"Yes, I'll marry you. I want to spend my life loving you."

"What about Kenny? Do you think he'll be okay with it?" Johnny asked. "I mean, he is man of the house."

She looked up at him with a twinkle in her eye. "I think he can wait a while to take over. He needs a big man around."

Then she kissed him so hard that he fell backward. Pain knifed through his chest, but he laughed anyway, then cupped her face in his hands and kissed her even deeper, hoping she felt the love in his heart.

He had come to the BBL to help troubled kids like he'd once been, but he'd found a second chance, himself.

A chance to have love and a family to call his own. And he would never let them go.

Epilogue

Johnny parked in front of the state pen, determined this time to help his friend, even if Carter didn't want it.

He stared up at the prison barbed wire with a grimace. God knows, he'd be crazy if he'd been locked up in here for five years. And maybe just as bitter as Carter.

He had looked back over the evidence the past few days and realized that Carter had had a shoddy defense.

And that the police had missed something.

Perspiration trickled down the back of his neck as he went into the prison, passed through security and took a seat in the visitors' room. This time, when Carter shuffled in, he looked even worse. Dark bruises, a jagged cut above his eye, a flat, hopeless expression as if he'd given up.

"What the hell are you doing here again?" Carter mumbled. "Thought the big, famous rodeo star would be off on his honeymoon."

Johnny ignored the barb. "I see you read the papers."

Carter stared down at his scarred hands folded on the table. "Looks like you and Brandon were big hits."

"For once, can it with the bitterness," Johnny snapped.

Carter's scowl deepened, but Johnny saw pain in his eyes. "What do you want, Johnny?"

"To get you out of here," Johnny said. "And like it or not, I'm going to help you."

Johnny removed a business card from his pocket and shoved it toward Carter, sliding it beneath the small opening in the Plexiglas. "This is the name of a P.I. I hired to look into your case."

Carter glanced at the card but didn't move to take it.

"He's going to contact you." Johnny stood. "Maybe he can dig up some new evidence to clear your name."

Johnny started to walk away, but Carter called his name, and Johnny turned back to him. Carter's hangdog expression twisted Johnny's heart.

"You really think this guy can help me?" Carter asked in a gruff voice.

Johnny hesitated, not wanting to offer false hope. Carter had had such an awful childhood, and then to spend years in a cell for a crime he hadn't committed, it was beyond unfair.

He must have gotten his hopes up a thousand times, only to have them crushed.

But something had been amiss at that trial. And after seeing how easily Rex Presley had manipulated the system to frame Rachel, made him wonder if someone had framed Carter.

"Yeah, I do." Emotions tinged his voice. "If someone set you up, Carter, it's time we exposed them for what they did so the right person can pay and you can go free."

Although, freeing him wouldn't give Carter back the years he'd lost. But clearing his name would give him back his self-respect and a chance to start over.

Carter released a long-suffering sigh and scrubbed a hand down his chin. His handcuffs rattled in the silence.

"There is something," Carter said in a gruff voice.

Johnny slid back into the stiff vinyl chair. "What?"

"Remember that Native American girl I told you I saw the night of the murder?"

Johnny nodded. The one who'd disappeared into thin air. The one no one else believed existed.

"She was at your rodeo," Carter said. "I saw her in the stands in one of the pictures in the paper."

Adrenaline flooded Johnny. "I'll call Leon as soon as I leave and tell him to get here ASAP."

He stood again, anxious to make the call. "Maybe he'll have you out soon."

A sliver of hope softened Carter's bleak expression, and Johnny prayed he wouldn't be disappointed again.

The only thing that would make him happier than marrying Rachel and making a family with her and Kenny was to see Carter clear his name and for all of them to be friends again.

* * * * *